"Just what i[s] you've got against me?"

Zara bit back the angry reply to Heath's question and said shortly, "I make a point of not having any social connections with business associates."

She tried to get out of the car, but Heath put a hand behind her neck and held her captive. His lips ravaged hers, bringing back memories of the past she could never forget. Raising his head, he said roughly, "Now do you remember me?"

"Yes," Zara said fiercely. "You haven't changed a bit." With one kiss Heath had melted the wall of ice that had frozen her feelings.

But above all other emotions there was hatred and the need to hurt him as he had hurt her seven years ago. To deal him a blow that he would remember always....

SALLY WENTWORTH began her publishing career at a Fleet Street newspaper in London, where she thrived in the hectic atmosphere. After her marriage, she and her husband moved to rural Hertfordshire, where Sally had been raised. Although she worked for the publisher of a group of magazines, the day soon came when her own writing claimed her energy and time. Her romance novels are often set in fascinating foreign locales.

Books by Sally Wentworth

HARLEQUIN PRESENTS
614—JILTED
629—SHATTERED DREAMS
662—THE LION ROCK
686—BACKFIRE
733—DARK AWAKENING
750—VIKING INVADER
814—THE WINGS OF LOVE
837—FATAL DECEPTION
862—THE HAWK OF VENICE
926—THE KISSING GAME
974—CAGE OF ICE
997—TIGER IN HIS LAIR

HARLEQUIN ROMANCE
2262—LIBERATED LADY
2310—THE ICE MAIDEN
2361—GARDEN OF THORNS

Don't miss any of our special offers. Write to us at the following address for information on our newest releases.

Harlequin Reader Service
901 Fuhrmann Blvd., P.O. Box 1397, Buffalo, NY 14240
Canadian address: P.O. Box 603,
Fort Erie, Ont. L2A 5X3

SALLY
WENTWORTH

passionate revenge

Harlequin Books

TORONTO • NEW YORK • LONDON
AMSTERDAM • PARIS • SYDNEY • HAMBURG
STOCKHOLM • ATHENS • TOKYO • MILAN

Harlequin Presents first edition January 1988
ISBN 0-373-11046-4

Original hardcover edition published in 1987
by Mills & Boon Limited

Copyright © 1987 by Sally Wentworth. All rights reserved.
Philippine copyright 1987. Australian copyright 1987.
Except for use in any review, the reproduction or utilization of
this work in whole or in part in any form by any electronic,
mechanical or other means, now known or hereafter invented,
including xerography, photocopying and recording, or in any
information storage or retrieval system, is forbidden without
the permission of the publisher, Harlequin Enterprises Limited,
225 Duncan Mill Road, Don Mills, Ontario, Canada M3B 3K9.

All the characters in this book have no existence outside the
imagination of the author and have no relation whatsoever to
anyone bearing the same name or names. They are not even
distantly inspired by any individual known or unknown to the
author, and all incidents are pure invention.

The Harlequin trademarks, consisting of the words
HARLEQUIN PRESENTS and the portrayal of a Harlequin,
are trademarks of Harlequin Enterprises Limited and are
registered in the Canada Trade Marks Office; the portrayal
of a Harlequin is registered in the United States Patent
and Trademarks Office.

Printed in U.S.A.

CHAPTER ONE

THE bells in the church across the park rang out joyfully, the sound carrying clearly on the cold night air. The noise disturbed Zara's concentration and she lifted her head from the papers she had been working on to listen and then glance at the slim gold watch on her wrist. But she hardly needed its corroboration to know that it was midnight. Midnight on New Year's Eve. She looked back at her desk, but her attention had gone and she angrily threw down her pen and walked over to the window, pulling back the curtain to look out.

The night was cold and frosty, the stars twinkling like iridescent diamonds in the clear black velvet sky. Millions of jewels, stretching into infinity, making her feel small and insignificant in comparison. 'Damn!' Zara swore aloud. Why did she always have to feel so low and depressed every New Year's Eve? She had given up celebrating them now, given up even the pretence of doing so. Too many memories always came flooding back, to make her feel bitter when she should be happy and make her want to cry when she should be laughing. But not cry with sadness—no, she had never felt that. But to cry out with rage and hatred and hurt.

Lifting her clenched fist, Zara hit it hard against the window frame, but she was angry with herself now, for not being able to forget. It had been so long ago—

exactly seven years ago tonight. And yet the hurt of rejection was still there, raw and bleeding. Seven years was a long time and so much had happened during those years. Zara looked out across the tree-lined square to the houses on the other side. There were lights showing in most of them, either because there were parties going on, or to give would-be burglars the impression that the owners were at home. She herself had had invitations to a dozen different parties but had turned them all down—she wasn't good company on New Year's Eve. Although she ought to have forgotten by now, or at least not feel the hurt so much.

I'm successful now, she told herself urgently, with enough money for almost anything I want. As if to prove it to herself, Zara looked round her study, at the beautiful antique desk at which she had been working and at the original paintings on the walls, every item carefully and lovingly selected to enhance the already rich but tasteful décor. Just to look round the room gave her comfort, but she opened the door and walked round the rest of the flat, through the large, high-ceilinged drawing-room decorated in green and gold, and on to the dining-room with its beautiful Regency table and ten matching chairs. These two rooms she used for entertaining, to give either intimate dinner parties or larger cocktail parties for friends or to further her company's interests. Although most of her friends, she realised, came from her business world; there were few that she had kept in touch with from her home town and none from the short time of her disastrous marriage.

Beyond the dining-room was the kitchen, a gleaming showpiece of white and chrome with every latest labour-saving machine, most of which she hardly ever used; her daily cleaner-cum-housekeeper, Mrs Nye, very efficiently taking care of all that side of things. But Zara had designed the layout of the kitchen herself, with the usual care and attention to detail that had made her such a success in business. Although the only gadget that she ever really used was the coffee-maker—that was in almost constant use when she was at home.

There were only two other rooms in the flat; her bedroom and the sumptuous bathroom opening off it. Zara had gone to town on the bathroom—if you couldn't have sybaritic luxury while you were having a bath, where could you have it? So she had had a sunken jacuzzi bath fitted and a shower that jetted first hot and then cold water, stinging her already slender body into healthy perfection. The main feature of the bedroom was a big four-poster bed that Zara had picked up in pieces at a country auction sale. One of her own craftsmen had restored it and she had designed the material for the hangings, curtains and bedspread and had it made up in the factory; an exclusive design used only for this room.

Yes, Zara thought with satisfaction, she had done well, everything was the best she could afford and pleasing to the eye. Some critics might say that she had veered towards the aesthetic rather than comfort, but she worked too hard to have much time for comfort anyway.

Feeling better, she went back into the study and was just drawing the curtain when the phone rang. She gave a small smile, knowing who it would be, and picked up the receiver, 'Hallo, Richard.'

He gave a warm laugh. 'Am I so predictable?'

'No, just reliable.'

'Hm, I wonder if that's good or bad. But anyway; happy New Year, darling.'

'And to you. Is it a good party?'

'It would be if you were here. Without you it's boring. Why don't you stop working for a couple of hours and come over? I'll send the car for you.'

'You know I can't do that, the end of the year is a busy time for me.'

'All work and no play, you know,' he wheedled.

'Are you saying that you find me dull, Richard?' Zara asked provocatively.

His voice changed, became thick. 'No, I find you damned exciting,' he admitted.

'Thank you. I may work hard, but I play hard too.'

'*And* hard to get,' he commented with irony. 'Why don't you make a New Year's resolution, Zara my darling—to agree to marry me, or at least for us to become lovers?'

It was Zara's turn to laugh. 'I always thought New Year resolutions made you *abstain* from excesses, not indulge in them!'

'And do you think we would indulge in excesses if we became lovers?' he asked meaningfully.

'Stop flirting, Richard—I have to get back to work. Enjoy the rest of your party.'

'I could come round there,' he offered with little hope.

'No, you couldn't.'

'Why not?'

There was a slight but unmistakable edge to Zara's voice. 'Because you haven't been invited. Goodnight, Richard. Thanks for phoning.' And she firmly put down the receiver over his protests.

Sitting down at her desk again, Zara picked up the silver pen that had been a present from Richard on her last birthday. Some time soon she was going to have to make her mind up about him. He was really becoming very persistent. Marriage of course was out of the question; she had sworn never to make that mistake again, but an affair ...? She toyed with the idea, wondering what he would be like in bed, but was suddenly disgusted with herself, knowing that she would never sleep with him. There was no excitement in the relationship, no need or desire—not on her part anyway, although she knew Richard felt exactly the opposite. He wanted her very badly and made no secret of it, had even proposed to her within three months of meeting her. He was successful, and good-looking in a moderate kind of way, the kind of man who made an ideal escort when she needed one, but it wasn't fair to keep him dangling like this. And she decided she liked him too much to attempt to have an unsuccessful affair with him, because Zara knew from experience that she would immediately start making comparisons and feel bitter because Richard, she knew instinctively, wouldn't come up to standard. But then her standards, she was beginning to believe, were impossibly high. And all because of one man, a man she had met on New Year's Eve, seven years ago tonight.

* * *

'You can't possibly stay at home by yourself on New Year's Eve!' Zara could hear her sister's voice now, echoing down the years. 'Just because Christopher is ill you don't have to stay home, too.' Denise had been into Women's Lib that year and she had been quite indignant, almost angry. 'Why don't you go to the disco on your own?'

'Oh no, I couldn't do that,' Zara had answered. 'Christopher wouldn't like it.' She could imagine his reaction if she told him—or if any of their friends told him. He would sulk for days if she went without him.

Denise glared at her. 'Honestly, Zara, I don't know why you bother with Christopher any more. Why don't you find yourself a new boy-friend?'

But that was easier said than put into practice. Zara had been going around with Christopher since she was thirteen, over five years, and neither of them had ever been out with anyone else. Childhood sweethearts, as Christopher's mother was fond of putting it.

'Never mind,' her own mother said placatingly. 'Christopher's nice enough. But Zara will probably meet lots of new people when she goes to university.'

'If I pass my exams,' Zara pointed out, crossing her fingers for luck. Not that it was necessary; they all knew she was the brightest pupil in her year and destined for a good university.

'Well, if you won't go to your teenage party why don't you come to the one I'm going to?' Denise persisted.

'But I won't know anyone,' Zara objected.

'I thought that was the whole idea. There won't be anyone who can sneak on you to Christopher. Come on, Zara,' cajoled Denise. 'You'll enjoy it. It's going to be a really good party. And I don't know that many people either, so I'll be glad of your company. Tell you what—I'll even let you choose something of mine to wear.'

Torn, Zara looked at her mother and sister, greatly tempted; she hated the idea of spending the evening alone. Even her mother and father were going out, so she wouldn't have their company either. Her mother added her voice to Denise's, so that in the end Zara gave way to her own inclinations and went upstairs to Denise's room to choose a dress. She tried on several but settled for a deep green velvet sheath dress that was much more sophisticated than she usually wore. But then Denise was six years older and worked in London, so she wore far more adult and fashionable clothes. Both girls had green eyes and red hair, but Denise's was bright, gingery red while Zara's was a darker, deep copper shade. Usually she wore it in a ponytail, but Denise insisted on washing and blow-drying it into a loose but very becoming style that came down to her shoulders and flicked back off her face.

'I might as well do your make-up for you, too,' Denise decided, enjoying herself. 'And your nails. Don't you ever paint them?'

'We're not allowed to at school. The teachers always make us go along to the first aid room and have it cleaned off.'

The two girls spent a very pleasant couple of hours getting themselves ready, and it wasn't until Denise had driven them over to the party, in a big house about twenty miles away, that Zara began to feel nervous.

'Are you sure it will be all right?' she asked worriedly. 'After all, I haven't been invited.'

'Of course it is. The Howards always hold open house on New Year's Eve. Everyone from the tennis club will be there. Tony Howard is the president, you know, and his wife is the secretary. And everyone's been told to bring a friend, so there'll be lots of people there they don't actually know. Come on, let's go in.'

Denise rang the bell and the door was opened by a middle-aged man who was dressed in clothes that were too young for him. 'Hallo, Denise darling. Come on in.' He gave Denise an eager kiss. 'And who's this?'

'My sister Zara. You did say to bring someone.'

'Of course—delighted. Hallo, Zara. Welcome to the Howard madhouse. Always pleased to have another beautiful girl along.'

He sounded fulsome to Zara, but when they went up to a bedroom to take off their coats and she looked at their reflections side by side in the mirror she changed her mind. Denise had made her up so skilfully that the two girls looked almost the same age. And she did look beautiful, Zara realised with a kind of wonder. Christopher's mother didn't approve of make-up, which meant that Christopher didn't either, so Zara never wore more than a touch of powder and pale pink lipstick, but Denise had done her work so well that her green eyes glowed and you could see the fine bone structure of her face, hidden before beneath freckles and a layer of puppy-fat that she hadn't bothered to try and get rid of. If anyone asks me how old I am, she decided, I'll tell them I'm twenty. She looked at herself again and saw the way the velvet clung to her figure.

No, maybe I'll make it twenty-two.

Downstairs the party was in full swing, although the doorbell kept ringing for the next hour or so as more guests arrived. Denise was greeted by several people from the tennis club, although she had only joined it at the end of the summer when she had found out that a doctor from the local hospital that she fancied belonged to it. He was on duty tonight and so couldn't be at the party, but Denise had got to know him and they had been out together a few times, although she hadn't yet got as far as bringing him home to meet her family.

There were some young people at the party, but they were mostly in a higher age group than Zara's. The Howards, Tony and Janet, hadn't any children and so they chose their friends among other couples at the tennis, squash or golf clubs. Plus a few neighbours in a similar income bracket. That most of the people here were upwardly mobile was evident from the elegant way the women were dressed. And quite a few of the men were wearing evening suits or else velvet suits and jackets of different colours with frilly dress shirts underneath.

Denise introduced her to everyone she knew and twice they were asked if they were twins, which definitely made Zara feel adult. And because she was treated as a sophisticated good-looking girl, she behaved like one, parrying flirtatious remarks instead of going into fits of embarrassed giggles as she would probably have done if she had been with her own girl friends. Someone brought her a drink and she was soon dancing in the Howards' big drawing-room, the lights turned low and the music up high.

Zara wasn't sure when she first became aware of
someone watching her. She had been at the party a
couple of hours and was getting hot in the velvet dress.
Already she had had several drinks to try to cool off,
but she just seemed to get hotter than ever. Ever since
she had arrived she seemed to have been dancing non-
stop, and she was dancing a fast beat number with a
friend of Denise when she felt a prickly sensation at the
back of her neck and turned to see a man standing over
by the french windows, a glass in his hand, his eyes
apparently fixed on her.

The movement of the dance made her turn away,
but she soon sneaked another glance as she whirled
round. The man was dressed in a well cut black
evening suit and was very tall and broad-shouldered.
About twenty-eight, a man, not a boy. Zara danced on
and gained an impression of him in a series of fast-
moving covert glances that built into a picture like the
pieces in a jigsaw puzzle. She saw the hard, clean-cut
lines of his face; a long capable hand holding his drink;
his slim, athletic waist; thick dark hair cut rather long;
an expensive gold watch on his wrist, a strong mouth
above the square jaw; and dark, long-lashed eyes that
slowly smiled as if he knew exactly what she was doing.

Her heart beating, not only from the energetic
jiving, Zara rejoined the group she was with and
carefully refrained from looking towards the french
windows again, although all her senses were alive to
the man standing there. Another round of drinks was
brought over and Zara drank hers thirstily, although it
tasted very dry.

'Only another ten minutes to midnight,' one girl said eagerly. 'What resolutions shall we make?'

'I know one I'd like to make,' a young man answered, looking meaningfully at Denise.

But her sister was more than a match for him. 'Resolutions are only for people who have no self-control—like you. That's why they're always broken.'

Everyone laughed, and Zara took the opportunity to walk over to a small table and put down her empty glass, turning so that she was facing the room and could see the french window again. The man was still there—but he had a girl with him. A short and pretty brunette who had her hands on his waist and was looking up at him provocatively, almost pleadingly. The man had a small, rather sardonic smile playing on his lips, as if it amused him to take the passive role and let the girl do the chasing. A flash of emotion she didn't even recognise as jealousy tore through Zara's slim body as she watched the unknown girl.

'Zara.' She turned quickly as someone thrust a squeaker and some streamers into her hands. For a moment she felt quite giddy, but then recovered as Tony Howard came round with a large tray loaded with glasses of champagne.

'Here you are—have to see the New Year in properly,' he told them, his voice slurring over the last word.

The record player was turned off and the radio tuned in to the commentator speaking from the celebrations in Trafalgar Square. Everyone crowded round as the commentator said, 'Only one minute to midnight now. Fifty seconds. Twenty. Ten, nine . . .'

They all began to chant with him. 'Eight, seven, six, five, four ...'

Zara felt oppressed by the crush and turned to fight her way out, waves of dizziness making her head swim. 'Three, two.'

Somebody took her arm and pushed people out of the way until she was clear of the crowd. '*ONE!*' everyone roared. 'Happy New Year!'

Zara took a deep breath of air and found herself looking up into the eyes of the man who had so attracted her attention. He was still holding her arm, but now he lifted his free hand with the glass of champagne in it and said in a low insinuating voice, 'Hallo. Happy New Year.'

For a moment Zara gazed at him, then, as if mesmerised, she lifted her own glass and clinked it against his. 'Happy New Year,' she said huskily, and they both drank, their eyes holding in a much deeper toast. The man smiled, then slid his arm round Zara's waist, drew her to him and kissed her. He kissed her gently at first, his lips exploring the sweet softness of hers. Zara gave a low sigh of pleasure and opened her mouth under his. She felt him give a small quiver of awareness, then his arm tightened, his kiss growing deeper and more insistent. Around them everyone was blowing squeakers, throwing streamers, kissing their friends and generally greeting the New Year as noisily and merrily as they could, but Zara and the man stood in a close circle of oblivion, unaware of the coloured streamers that landed on their heads and shoulders, deaf to the noise and the people. It was only when everyone joined into a big circle to sing Auld Lang

Syne that he released her, smiling down into her wide eyed face for a moment before taking her glass from her so that they too could join in the circle.

Zara sang and laughed with the rest of them, but was only really aware of the man's hand holding hers in a firm grip, of his height when she was so tall herself, of his dark eyes that looked often into hers, and of his mouth with that slightly twisted smile on his lips. Lips that had given her so much pleasure that it made her feel lightheaded, almost as if she were two people; the one who was a part of the laughing, linked throng and the one who was just marking time until he kissed her again.

By the time the song was ended everyone was exhausted, so Tony Howard put a slow, smoochy record on to give them time to recover. Without even thinking about it, Zara turned to the man and lifted her arms so that he could put his around her and hold her close as they began to dance. His lips curved into that lazy smile as he said, 'Hallo again. You haven't told me your name.'

'It's Zara—Zara Layston.'

'Zara. I like that.' He bent to gently kiss her ear-lobe. 'And I'm beginning to like you—very much.'

Zara gave a little gasp and squirmed deliciously, loving the sensations he was arousing in her. She stumbled a little and laughed with him as he held her. 'And you haven't told me your name,' she pointed out.

'I'm Heath Masterson. Our hosts didn't do a very good job of introducing everyone, did they? I shall have to tell Tony off for not introducing me to the loveliest girl in the room.'

For a moment Zara wondered who he meant and then flushed with pleasure as she realised he was talking about her. She gave him a quick, shy glance and saw from the mocking look in his eyes that he was only flirting with her, he didn't really mean it. She relaxed a little and smiled, rather relieved that he wasn't being serious. 'Do you know the Howards well?' she asked him.

'No, not terribly. Tony is a business acquaintance. I've been to a couple of his parties before, and as I'm staying in the neighbourhood over the holiday, he invited me along tonight. His wife I hardly know at all.'

'Oh, really?' Zara gave him an interested look, having already heard from Denise something of their hosts' open-marriage lifestyle.

Heath laughed, guessing her thoughts, his dark eyes gleaming with amusement. 'No, I don't. And anyway, a gentleman doesn't ever kiss and tell.' And, as if to emphasise his words, he sought her lips and lightly kissed her again.

His kiss had the strangest effect on her senses; she would have liked it to go on much, much longer. As it was she stood still, but another couple bumped into them and Heath deftly moved her out of the way and went on dancing.

'How about you?' he asked. 'Are you a friend of Janet's? Or of Tony's?' he added after a deliberate pause.

'Of neither,' Zara admitted with a laugh. 'I don't really know them at all. I've never been here before. They're friends of my sister, from the tennis club. I was at a loose end tonight, so I came along to the party with her.'

'I'm very glad you did,' Heath murmured, and held her closer as they went on dancing.

To Zara it was heady stuff; only ever having been out with Christopher before, she wasn't used to being complimented or treated like a woman instead of a girl. And Heath Masterson was so self-possessed and confident, wearing his arrant masculinity as easily as his beautifully cut dinner-suit. And he made her feel so deliciously feminine and sophisticated herself. It went to her head far more potently than the wine she had been drinking, just as his nearness aroused exciting sensations that she had never felt with Christopher.

But it was so hot in the room. Little beads of perspiration glowed on Zara's forehead and she wished now that she had chosen something cooler than velvet. When the dance ended Heath looked down at her and said firmly, 'We need a drink.' Taking her by the hand, he led her into the dining-room where a hired waiter was dispensing drinks at a bar which had been built into a recess. 'What would you like?'

Zara would have loved a long, cold drink like iced lemonade, but thought that that sounded childish, so she said, 'White wine, please.'

It was a little cooler in here but not much, and the chairs had all been taken by the older people who tended to stick in groups, so there was nowhere they could sit.

Heath emerged from the small crowd round the bar carrying two glasses and a bottle of wine that was so cold it misted over as she looked at it. He gave a glance

round and said, 'Let's find somewhere cooler. Let me
see, I think I remember . . .' Taking her arm, he led her
out into the hall and into a room opening off it that
looked like a small television room, but opening off
that were double doors leading into a conservatory
furnished with a comfortable sofa and armchairs,
where the Howards probably spent a lot of time in the
summer. Even here it was still warm, the heating kept
on to preserve all the pot plants, but compared to the
big party room it was delightfully cool.

'Oh, that's much better!' Zara sighed thankfully.

'Good. And now some wine to quench your thirst.'
Heath gave her a glass and sat down on the sofa. 'How
about joining me?'

She went willingly enough, kicking off her shoes to
tuck her feet under her.

Heath put a casual arm along the back of the settee
and her heart skipped a beat, but he made no attempt
to touch her. 'Do you live near here?' he asked. 'I
suppose you must if your sister belongs to the local
tennis club.'

'Yes, in Meeston. And you?'

He shook his head. 'No, I live in London. I work for
an advertising firm there. Or at least I do at the
moment, I'm in the process of negotiating another job.
I usually spend Christmas with an elderly aunt who
lives a few miles away, but I stretched my visit until
tomorrow so that I could come to the party.' He picked
up her hand and began to play with her fingers. 'And
I'm beginning to be very glad I did,' he added, his dark
eyes smiling down into hers.

Zara's pulses began to race. Unskilled as yet in the

art of flirtation, she answered with husky sincerity, 'So am I.'

The flippant riposte he was about to make died in Heath's throat, an arrested expression replacing the mockery in his eyes. Lifting a long finger, he stroked the side of her cheek caressingly and ran it across her lips, the bottom one trembling with the fullness of unawakened sexuality. 'And what do you do?' he asked gently. 'You haven't told me.'

'Oh, I don't do anything much,' Zara prevaricated, not wanting to tell him that she was still at school. 'At the moment I've got a job in a local department store.' But she didn't add that it was only until the Christmas holidays ended, a temporary job helping out during the January sales.

Even here they could clearly hear the music from the party, and Heath got to his feet. 'Let's dance,' he suggested, holding out his hand to her.

It felt so right in his arms; Zara could feel the strength of his muscles through his sleeves, smell the faint but insinuative tang of his aftershave, and was more than aware of his hard body whenever it touched hers. Which was often. He seemed to enjoy holding her close as much as she did. He talked to her as they moved slowly around the room, about the record that was being played and music in general, drawing her out to give her own opinions and making her laugh when he told her about a video advertising film he had been involved in that featured a well known group. 'So in the end the hotel refused to take them any more and we had to house them in a caravan at the back of the recording studio,' he finished.

Zara laughed delightedly. 'Oh, I do wish I'd been there to see it!' She looked at him wistfully. 'Your job sounds terribly exciting. Do you get to meet many show-biz stars?'

'A few. Mostly actors and actresses who come to do voice-overs—you know, the background voice that tells you about the product while the ad is going on. We don't get to meet so many pop stars.'

He let her go to refill their glasses with the wine, which wasn't so cool and thirst-quenching now. 'Are you going to make any New Year resolutions?' he asked.

Zara shook her head with a rueful smile. 'I never seem able to keep them. Are you?'

Heath gave a small smile, his eyes warm and flirting again. 'Oh, I think there's one I will definitely have to make.' And he drew her towards him to kiss her neck.

She lifted her head on a small gasp of pleasure, wondering why it had never felt so good before. 'I like that,' she breathed.

His eyebrows rising slightly, Heath found her lips and kissed her properly, moulding her slim body to his. When Christopher kissed her he used his tongue to force her mouth open, and seemed to feel that the deeper he thrust in his tongue the more passionate was the kiss and the more she would like it. Zara had got used to this gauche and insensitive treatment, so that it came as quite a revelation when Heath kissed her gently, with little kisses that moved over her lips, exploring their softness, teasing and insinuating, rousing her senses to a new level of excitement. For Zara the kiss could have gone on for ever, but all too soon Heath raised his head and stepped away from her, taking a long swallow of his drink. Shaking his head a little, he said, 'Wow! I think we'd better go back to the party before things get too heavy, don't you?'

Zara didn't entirely agree, but she nodded anyway, and Heath put his arm round her waist as he led her back through the house. The music had really hotted up again and Heath immediately took her on to the floor to dance, moving easily to the beat, and clearly enjoying himself as much as she was.

Within five minutes Zara was as hot as ever again, and as the music ended and they waited for someone to change the record, she raised her arms to lift the heavy fall of chestnut hair off her neck. Heath had just lifted his glass to his mouth, but he paused with it in mid-air as he looked at her, his eyes frankly admiring. 'You look sensational when you do that.'

This time his voice had been entirely sincere and Zara's cheeks, already flushed with heat, went an even deeper red. 'Thank you,' she answered, feeling stupidly tongue-tied and embarrassed. 'Would you—would you like to meet my sister?'

Heath's eyes grew mocking again, but he nodded, 'Of course. Which one is she? Let me guess.' He looked round the room and focused on the group where Denise stood. 'That must be her,' he pointed. 'She's the only other redhead in the room.'

They strolled over and Zara saw that Denise's doctor friend had managed to get there. He was standing with a proprietorial arm round her waist, a glass in his other hand, his laughter fighting away the lines of tiredness around his eyes. Denise glanced up as they came over and a rather guilty look came into her eyes, so Zara guessed that she had forgotten all about her promise to their mother to keep an eye on her. Her eyes widened when she saw Heath and she lifted a beckoning hand. 'Hallo. Are you having a good time? You remember Peter, don't you?'

'Yes, of course. Hallo. Happy New Year.'

'Thanks.' Peter leaned forward and gave her a peck on the cheek.

Denise was looking at her expectantly, so Zara, her voice a little shaky with a mixture of shyness and pride, said, 'This is Heath Masterson. We—er—just met.'

'Hallo.' Denise shook hands with Heath and looked him over in open appraisal and with all the confidence of her twenty-four years. She began to talk to him, but Zara's attention was diverted by Peter, who asked her if she had had a good Christmas.

The conversation became general for a while until Tony Howard came in and announced that they were going to play some games. Zara thought that Heath would be bored by the idea, but he joined in willingly enough, always close beside her. In one game she had to sit on his lap, which she found extremely sensuous— and Heath didn't seem to mind in the least either. Another game entailed the girls all having to put on one of the men's jackets and then run outside. Zara was swamped by Heath's jacket and found it almost impossible to run very fast in the velvet dress so that Heath caught her easily. She was bubbling with laughter and from the heady excitement of being chased, so that Heath burst into laughter too, and swung her up in his arms, whirling round with her to make her shriek and cling to him, her arms around his neck. He kissed her then, hard on the mouth, a real kiss of masculine desire and domination.

Zara gazed up at him speechlessly, her eyes wide with surprise at her own awakened sensuality.

The party went on all night, but it quietened down quite a lot towards morning. Those who were left danced desultorily or sat around and talked. Heath sat in an armchair with Zara on his lap, occasionally running his finger idly down the long column of her throat or brushing his cheek against the softness of her hair. At seven they came alive again to eat breakfast, washed down with champagne, in the Howards' farmhouse-style kitchen, and at eight Heath took her home, leaving Denise with Peter.

Zara didn't feel in the least tired; she felt light and bubbly as air, like the bubbles that had jumped out of the champagne glass and tickled her nose. She made Heath laugh as they drove home through the cold morning, the trees made beautiful as the sunlight glinted on the layers of frost that clung to the branches. She was too exhilarated to feel cold, but when they drew up outside her house she pretended to be, so that Heath pulled her close to him to keep her warm.

He kissed her again and rubbed her nose with his, making her laugh. 'Thank you, Zara,' he said softly, 'for making the year start so happily. I hadn't expected to enjoy that party, but you really made it for me.'

'And you for me. It was the best party I've ever been to,' she told him exuberantly.

He grinned and ran his hand through her hair. 'I wish now that I hadn't arranged to go back to London today.' He kissed the tip of her nose. 'Would I be treading on anyone's toes if I asked you to come out with me?'

'Treading . . .? Oh, I see.' Realising what he meant, Zara gave one quick guilty thought to Christopher before consigning him into the past. 'No, no one special.'

'Good.' Heath kissed her ear. 'So will you come?'

'To—to London?' she asked breathlessly.

'If you could. It only takes about an hour or so on the train. Or I could come down here, if you like?'

'No, I'd like to come to London. There are so many more places to go there.'

'That's true,' he agreed with a grin. 'So when can you come?'

They arranged for Zara to travel up straight from work in two days' time, then kissed again before she went reluctantly indoors, to crawl into bed and lie awake, gazing up at the ceiling, remembering, her heart whirling with excitement and happiness. Nothing like this had ever happened to her before and she was intoxicated by it, by Heath's evident admiration and interest as well as by her own awakened awareness. She felt as if she wanted to be a woman now, not a girl any more. She wanted to be sophisticated and beautiful, poised and self-assured. For Heath, all for Heath. Her thoughts went forward to seeing him again and she fell asleep with a happy smile of anticipation on her lips.

Christopher's mother rang the next day to say that his illness had turned out to be mumps, and as Zara had never had it, her own mother forbade her to go round and see him, which suited Zara very well at the moment. She had been going around with Christopher for so long that not seeing him was like being given a taste of freedom. And she was enjoying the taste, especially as she had met Heath. He was so much more adult, so much more exciting to be with. Only now was she beginning to realise that Christopher had become a habit and that her feelings for him were only of friendship after all. But they had shared so much and he was so keen on her that Zara didn't want to hurt him, so this illness had come just at the right time, she could put off telling him until he was better.

Heath took her out for a meal in an Italian restaurant, and on to the theatre; the table booked in advance, good seats in the stalls and drinks waiting for them in the bar at the interval. Zara enjoyed the play, but was unable to give it her whole attention because Heath held her hand. That, and because she kept stealing glances at him to make sure that she was really here and wasn't dreaming. After the theatre he took her to the station to catch her train and arranged to see her again at the weekend before kissing her goodbye very satisfactorily.

This time he drove down to stay with his aunt again so that they were able to spend most of the time together, only the icy weather a bar to their enjoyment. It was even too cold to sit in the car and kiss goodnight for more than ten minutes. But on the Sunday afternoon Heath's aunt went out to visit a friend and so they were able to go back to her flat and sit on the floor in front of the fire, toasting crumpets which they layered with butter for their tea. Afterwards Heath sat on the settee and pulled her down on to his lap.

Zara went very willingly, her arms going round his neck as he kissed her avidly, not releasing her mouth until her heart was beating crazily and her body was on fire with sensations that threatened to drown her. She stared at him, her chest heaving, and said, 'Oh!' on a long note of discovery.

His eyes darkening, Heath held her for a long moment, then bore her back against the arm of the settee to kiss her again with the expertise that can only come from experience, sending Zara's senses reeling as she returned his embrace, wanting to give as well as to take. His hands ran over her, making her breath catch in her throat, but he made no attempt to do more, although his kisses grew more passionate.

At length he sat up abruptly and held her away from him, his breathing unsteady. 'You minx,' he said huskily. 'Do you know what you're doing to me?'

As she was sitting on his lap, Zara had quite a good idea. She gave a breathless, uncertain laugh and sat up, lifting her hair away from her hot skin at her neck.

'Mm, you look beautiful when you do that. Here, let me.'

Heath replaced her hands with his, letting her hair run through his fingers. 'Lord, I wish . . .' He broke off and shook his head. 'It doesn't matter.'

He took her home shortly afterwards and then drove back to London, but they went out together twice during the following week and again at the weekend. The weather was a bit milder now, although it had snowed during the week and the snow still lay on the ground, crisp and white in the sunlight. They put on lots of clothes and went for a walk in a neighbouring park, leaving trails of footsteps in the snow behind them.

'I had to go to another interview on Friday for that new job I'm trying for,' Heath told her. 'They've narrowed it down to a short list of four people now.'

'Why, that's marvellous,' Zara enthused. 'I'm sure you'll get it.'

'Thanks for the vote of confidence. But it will mean quite a few changes.' He gave her a rather troubled, speculative look. 'Do you like travelling, Zara? Abroad, I mean?'

'Yes, I suppose so. But I've only ever been to Europe on school trips and for holidays with my parents. I enjoyed those.'

'Have you ever thought about leaving home—working abroad?'

She shook her head in surprise. 'Why, no. Do you mean as an au pair, or something?'

'Sort of. It doesn't matter.' He shrugged dismissively. 'Come on, race you to the top of the hill.'

He beat her, of course, and had a handful of snow waiting to try and put down her neck when she finally caught him up. Zara shrieked and they had a wonderful game, tumbling and sliding in the snow, until they fell over together and Heath couldn't resist kissing her cold lips as he lay on top of her. 'Oh, Zara, Zara,' he said huskily. 'How I wish I'd met you before!'

But then he rolled off her and was making her run and slide down the hill again before she could ask him what he meant.

He was as reluctant to leave that weekend as Zara

was to have him go. They clung together in the car outside her house on Sunday evening, not wanting to part.

'I'll phone you tomorrow,' Heath promised. 'And you'll come up to London on Wednesday?'

'Yes, of course. Oh, Heath!' She nestled close in his arms, wanting to hold him beside her for ever. He kissed her hungrily and almost had to push her out of the car, laughing ruefully as he did so.

'Lord, I don't want to leave you. But I must; I have to travel up to Manchester early tomorrow morning, and if I don't leave now I won't get any sleep at all.'

So they parted reluctantly and Zara had to face the dreary reality of getting her things together to start the new term the next day. She had never felt less like continuing her education. Somehow it all seemed superfluous now that she had met Heath. She was head over heels in love with him and realised that she had been from the moment she first saw him. She had often read of men falling in love at first sight and it seemed that it could happen to women too. It certainly had to her, and she fell even deeper in love with him with each passing day, her heart jumping crazily every time she saw him. And he treated her so well, admittedly having more money to spend than Christopher, but he was so attentive too, always helping her with her coat, opening the car door for her, and putting a protective hand under her elbow when they crossed the road. He treated her as if she was very special and made her feel admired and cherished. With Christopher, although she hadn't acknowledged it before, she had come to feel as if she were his possession, the way he always

introduced her as 'my girl-friend' without even
bothering to add her name.

She got into trouble when she went back to school
because she had been supposed to work on a project
during the holidays but hadn't had the time or the
motivation to do it. And Christopher's mother had
phoned several times to ask why she hadn't been round
to enquire about him or even rung and asked. And
then her own mother started asking her about Heath
and told her she wanted to meet him. She also forbade
Zara to go out with him during the week now that she
was back at school and studying for her advanced
exams in the summer. But Zara pointed out that she
was eighteen and could do what she liked, which led to
a row with both her parents.

Defying them, she went up to London to meet Heath
on Wednesday, meeting him at the station as usual.
There was an air of excitement about him, although he
didn't say anything until they were seated in the
Italian restaurant again and he ordered champagne to
go with their meal.

'Champagne?' Zara's eyebrows rose. 'Are we
celebrating?'

'We are indeed,' Heath answered with a big grin.
'I've been offered that new job.'

'Why, that's marvellous! I told you you'd get it,
didn't I? Tell me all about it.'

'Later. I thought we might go round to my flat after
we've eaten—listen to some music or something.'

Zara looked quickly into his face, her heart jumping
crazily when she saw the warmth in his eyes. Her voice
catching in her throat, she said, 'I'd like that.' Then she

hastily lifted her glass. 'Here's to your new job. Congratulations.'

'Thanks, but I haven't accepted it yet. I have until the end of the month to decide.'

He went on to talk of other things during the meal, but the food was largely wasted as far as Zara was concerned; her stomach was so tight with anticipation that she could hardly eat a thing. Heath had never suggested going back to his flat before, and she longed to be alone with him but felt shy and a little afraid too, wondering what he intended. So far he had done nothing more than kiss and caress her, but Zara had already begun to feel that that wasn't enough, his kisses aroused her sensuousness to such heights of desire that her body craved to be loved. Physically she was ready for fulfilment and emotionally she was very much in love.

It was cold outside and they ran to the car, Zara wearing her new high-heeled boots that had been a Christmas present from Denise and having to cling to Heath's arm so that she didn't slip on the icy pavement. They were both in a happy mood and laughed a lot during the short drive to Heath's flat in Knightsbridge, not far from Harrods. But when they reached it Zara grew shy again until Heath kissed her in laughing surprise. She forgot everything else then, everything but the joyous magic of being close to him, of feeling his lips warm and demanding against hers. As he kissed her, Heath unbuttoned her coat and slid it from her shoulders to the floor. His arms tightened around her and his shoulders hunched as his kiss deepened to passion. 'Zara,' he murmured against her neck. 'My darling girl!' Leading her over to a big leather chesterfield, he drew her down beside him and kissed her again before sighing and saying, 'Lord, I wish I'd met you a few months earlier.'

'Why? What do you mean?' Zara's eyes were half closed, her head on his shoulder.

'Because I want this new job very badly, it's the kind of opening I've been working for ever since I started in advertising. But it means . . .' His hands tightened on her shoulders and he held her a little away from him. 'It means that I'll have to leave England and go to America.'

'America!' Zara sat up and looked at him in consternation.

'Yes, I'm afraid so. To New York. That's why I wish that we'd met earlier.'

'Why? What difference would it have made?' She was staring at him, her heart frozen in fear.

'Well, if we'd known each other longer, if we were more sure of how we felt about each other, then I could ask you to come with me, but as it is we've known each other for such a short time that . . .'

'But I'm sure about how I feel about you,' Zara broke in impetuously. 'I—I'm in love with you—and I want to go with you. Oh, Heath, take me with you. *Please*! I—I couldn't bear it if you didn't.' There were tears of anxiety in her eyes and she was clutching him, almost shaking him in her eagerness.

'Zara, sweetheart!' Heath took hold of one of her hands and carried it to his lips. 'That's wonderful to hear, but how can you be so sure? I . . .'

'I am. *I am*!' she insisted. 'I love you very much.'

She gazed anxiously into his face, willing him to believe her, and he slowly lifted up a hand to caress her face, his eyes intent. 'You realise that we'd be living together?'

'Yes.' Her hands tightened. 'I want that.'

'Oh God, so do I!' Heath pulled her close and held her tightly, then kissed her with a fierce hunger that he hadn't shown before. 'What about your parents?' he asked. 'Will it be all right with them?'

Zara knew it would be far from all right with them, but she lied and said, 'Yes, don't worry about them. I'll—I'll talk to them.'

'Perhaps I ought to come and see them and . . .'

'No!' she said sharply. 'I'll deal with them—you don't have to see them.'

He frowned. 'But . . .'

But she put her lips against his to kiss away his objections. 'When will we leave?' she asked at length.

'Towards the middle of February, I should think. I have to give a month's notice to my present employers but I have some holiday leave due to me so we could go earlier and spend the time finding somewhere to live.' He hugged her in exhilarated excitement. 'It's going to be fantastic! The new job—and you.' His eyes darkened with desire. 'Why don't you come up to London again this weekend? Stay with me here so that we can spend the whole night together?' He smiled. 'And probably the whole day as well?'

Zara's heart jumped with excitement and longing. 'Oh, yes. Oh, yes, Heath, my darling!' And she went happily into his arms to seal the promise with a kiss of deep and heartfelt love.

Her parents, of course, were furious when she told them the next day, her father especially, and they ended up having a humdinger of a row. But Zara was quite adamant, obstinately refusing to listen to their arguments, saying that her mind was made up and she was going. Her heart was full of guilt, knowing the plans they had for her and knowing how much she was hurting and disappointing them, but this guilt only made her more bullishly obstinate in the false hope that it would shorten the rows and heartache.

'There's no way I'm going to let you go and live with some stranger,' her father declared furiously. 'Let alone leave the country.'

'You can't stop me! I'm eighteen and I'm going.'

It ended by her running upstairs in tears and locking herself in her bedroom. But it would be all right tomorrow. Tomorrow, Heath would phone and she would have the reassurance of his voice to know that she was right to persist in going with him.

He didn't ring. She never heard from him again. She tried to reach him, of course, tried frantically, but he had never got round to giving her his home address or telephone number, always having rung her, so there was no way that she could get in touch with him. Her only contact with him was the Howards, but when she rang and later went round to see them, Tony Howard was very evasive and said that he only knew Heath's business number, but then refused to give it to her or the name of his company. Zara begged and pleaded with him, and came the closest she had ever known to despair when he went on refusing. Desperate, Zara went up to London and tried to find his flat, walking the streets around Harrods all day long, but it had been dark that night and she just couldn't recognise his building, there were so many that looked alike. When she was at home she refused to go to school or go out for a week, and she sat by the phone the whole time, hoping every time it rang that it was Heath.

It wasn't until over a month had gone by and she knew that Heath must have left for America that Zara admitted to herself the bitter truth, that he had just changed his mind and decided not to take her after all. By then her puppy fat had been worn away by anxiety and she had become withdrawn and brooding. She no longer refused to go back to school; although the thought of university had no attraction for her now and she began to hate her home, wishing herself away from her parents who were being over-kind and conciliatory towards her.

She could only think that Heath must have been frightened off by her keenness and telling him that she loved him, which made her feel cheap. She also felt spurned and rejected, her confidence shattered, unable to believe that Heath could be cruel enough to lift her to the heights of happy expectation only to drop her without a word. Without a note or a phone call. Nothing. He didn't even care about her that much.

Disappointment and despair changed to bitterness and hatred, and coincided with a weekend when Christopher came home from university and came round to see her. He knew nothing about Heath, and Zara turned to him as if he could save her from drowning. Here at least was someone who liked and cared for her, who wanted her and with whom there was absolutely no fear of rejection. He was twenty, only two years older, but no match for Zara, whose determination and resolve was now backed by even stronger emotions. By the end of that weekend she had persuaded him that she had kept away from him because she wanted to make up her mind about her future, and now she had, deciding that she definitely didn't want to continue her education and she intended to get a job. And it wasn't difficult to persuade him also into marrying her straight away so that she could help to keep him while he finished *his* education.

She had made the right appeal; Christopher liked the good things in life, but his mother was a widow and couldn't always provide what he wanted, so it would be useful to have a wife working for him as well. He agreed, and they were married in May, much against her parents' wishes. They begged her to take her exams, which she did, but she refused all their entreaties to her to go on to university and seemed utterly defeated when she insisted on marrying Christopher.

The marriage hadn't worked out, of course. It was doomed from the start. How could it be otherwise when she was still hopelessly in love with Heath and couldn't help but compare the two men all the time? She had tried to conceal it, tried hard, but after two years they had separated and divorced. A time of emotional hell for which she took the entire blame because she had married Christopher on the rebound.

Zara shuddered, determined not to think of that time. It was long over. Looking down at the pen in her hand, she saw that she was holding it like a dagger, and wished suddenly that she had Heath's broad back to plunge it into. That New Year's Eve seven years ago, when she had the misfortune to meet him, had ruined not only her life but also Christopher's for a while. Yes, she would very much like the opportunity to take her revenge on Heath Masterson for the hurt he had done her, because only by retribution could she strike him from her mind for ever.

CHAPTER TWO

THE first meeting of the board of Webster & Layston for that year was called for ten-thirty in the morning on the following Monday. It was to be quite an important meeting to decide what form of promotion they should use to advertise the new range of sportswear that Zara had introduced. She had her own ideas, of course, she always had, but her team of fellow directors and managers were a young and lively group who often came up with ideas themselves, and she was always receptive.

At ten twenty-five Zara checked her appearance in the private cloakroom opening off her office. As usual she wore an outfit from their own range of extremely smart and fashionable clothes for executive women. This morning she had chosen a pale grey suit with a short box jacket and straight skirt, with a double-collared blouse in a soft emerald colour that exactly matched her eyes. With it she wore high-heeled black patent shoes and a wide matching belt that accentuated her very slender waist. Clothes were important, not only to Zara as a fashionable woman, but also for her image as the managing director and driving force behind the very successful and progressive company of Webster & Layston, known throughout the retail trade as Panache. Satisfied, Zara went back into the beautifully furnished and thickly carpeted room that looked more like a sitting-room than an office, picked up her briefcase containing all the relevant papers she needed and walked through into her secretary's much more functional office.

Her secretary was a man, a fact which most people seemed to find surprising, expecting her to be a feminist and to have nearly all women on her staff. But Zara had no sexual prejudices—as far as work was concerned—and always chose the best person for the job regardless of gender. Peter Mackenzie, whom everyone called Mac, was extremely good at his job and had proved extremely useful on more than one occasion, especially in the early days, when reps whose goods she had turned down had either turned nasty or tried to seduce her, mistakenly believing that her youth and looks would make her a pushover. Which she definitely wasn't!

Mac was ready, and after a brief word they walked down the corridor to the boardroom where the rest of the company's directors were waiting. They all stood up as Zara entered—men and women alike, which Zara hoped was a token of respect and friendship as well as good manners. She took her seat at the head of the long oak table, wished them a smiling good morning and got right down to business.

There were a few other items to be dealt with before the major item on the agenda: the promotion of the new range of 'Game, Set and Match' sportswear, but these were quickly dealt with and Zara looked over at her financial director. 'Harry, how much can we budget for the sportswear promotion? And for how long a period?'

'About a quarter of a million, I should think. But it will have to be carefully co-ordinated.'

'Of course.' Zara smiled around at them. 'It will have to be a team effort.'

They grinned or smiled back, all as keen and enthusiastic as she was. 'If we could open the new shop in Norwich to correspond with the advertising it might help,' someone suggested.

Zara nodded. 'Good idea.' She looked towards her marketing manager, Colin Royce. 'Have you got any ideas yet on which advertising agency to use?'

'Well, there's the company we used on our last promotion, of course. I know they'd be very keen to do it. And so would their biggest rivals. But there's a relatively new company that I think might come up with some very interesting ideas. It's called Masterads, and although it only started up about two years ago, has done some really eye-catching work.'

'All right,' Zara decided. 'Why don't you approach all three? Give them a month to come up with some basic ideas.'

They discussed the subject further, formulating their campaign, then broke for a buffet lunch which they ate in an adjoining room. Immediately after lunch Zara left for Rochester and Canterbury with the company's property manager to look at opportunities for opening new shops in those towns. The shops didn't bear the Webster & Layston name, of course, they came under the much more trendy name of Panache. The manager drove down while Zara sat in the back of the car and worked, dictating into a miniature cassette player or using the car-phone and by single-minded concentration managing to get a great deal done. Although she delegated to a large extent, Zara made sure she kept closely in touch with everything that happened in the company, and it was this attention to detail that had made her so successful.

She had first gone to work at Webster Textiles, as it was then known, after she had refused to go on to university, and had kept the job on after she had divorced Christopher. Her original post had been as general dogsbody, making the tea and running all the errands, but the owner, Mr Webster, was becoming elderly and, as he had no children, had no real interest in running the company. It made various materials to order, but when his Sales Manager left, Mr Webster couldn't be bothered to go out and get new orders, and so the place ran down and more staff left. Zara found herself in the position of office girl Friday, having to do a hundred and one different jobs, from doing the accounts to dealing with customers. It made her angry to see a good firm going to waste, and on her own initiative she went out and got them some new orders. Then she began to chivvy and bully Mr Webster into a renewed interest which gradually grew as he realised how single-minded Zara was about putting the company back on its feet.

While Christopher was away at university, Zara went to evening classes nearly every night of the week, taking courses in accounting, textile design, business studies, marketing and office management. It all helped with her job which she very much wanted to keep, and it also took her mind off what she already knew was a failing marriage. Marrying Christopher on the rebound had been the biggest mistake of her life, and she knew that eventually they would split up and she would have to earn her own living. Christopher stayed on at university an extra year and Zara quite happily gave up a large portion of her salary to him, but on the day he finished his education they parted, with hatred and resentment on his part and relief on hers.

But by then Websters was not only back on its feet but was expanding rapidly. Mr Webster began to look upon her as the child he had never had, and he taught her all he knew, his step more sprightly with the new lease of life she had given him. Between them they took the firm into the women's clothes market, combining with an established firm to make up-market garments out of their own materials. They then took over this firm, enabling Zara to have more say in the designs, and then went into knitwear and separates so that they could open a shop in which all the clothes bore their own label.

This was quite a gamble and took a lot of work, but by now Zara had no other interest. She lived and breathed Panache and all it stood for, the exhausting but exhilarating work filling the deep void of loneliness and rejection. The shop was a huge success, and on the day they opened their tenth Mr Webster retired to marry an equally sprightly widow and enjoy the autumn of his life. He and Zara had long been in partnership, but now she was in sole charge of what was rapidly becoming an empire, for their shops not only sold women's clothes but men's too, concentrating on smart business and casual clothes for the executive and fashion-conscious market—the type of clothes Zara liked to wear herself and to see the men around her in. And now they were widening their scope into sportswear for the growing leisure market, and Zara had her heart set on expanding into fittings for the home for people who had grown tired of the 'country garden' vogue that had been in for so long. There was bound to be an about-turn of taste before very long and Zara was determined to take full advantage of it, if not to create the about-turn herself.

Her time was, as usual, extremely well filled; she worked hard but she played hard too, going every Saturday morning to a Pineapple health club to work out, and quite often going out with Richard or one of the other men who were more than happy to act as her escort. But Richard she began to discourage; he was becoming too serious, and she had neither the time nor the inclination to settle down and become domestic-ated. Besides, she was still only twenty-five and there were lots more ambitions she had yet to fulfil. On the day she had left Christopher she had determined to become a millionairess by the time she was thirty; she had not only done it by the time she was twenty-five but had repeated it several times over. No, she had no time for marriage, and very little for men except as colleagues, or escorts when she needed one.

It was just over three weeks after the board meeting that Colin Royle, the marketing manager, asked to see her and brought in a large folio to put on her desk.

'You know that new advertising company we approached on the sportswear promotion? Well, they've sent in some ideas already—and they're good.

Take a look at these.'

Zara did so with growing interest; the ideas were for advertising on a local basis in the areas around their shops rather than for a nationwide campaign. 'As we only sell in our own shops Masterads suggest a great deal of nationwide advertising would be wasted and the money better spent with local campaigns geared to each area. And they don't suggest just the usual sports sponsorship but have come up with some really original ideas,' he added enthusiastically.

'Mm, I'm inclined to agree. What sort of terms and timing do they offer?'

'They're good too. They would organise everything to coincide with the goods going into the shops at the beginning of May in time for the summer. Look, they've detailed everything here. They seem extremely well organised.'

Zara smiled at Colin's keenness. 'So they do, but it won't do any harm to wait until the other two companies let us have their ideas. But I'd like to talk to the head of Masterads. Is there one person or is it a group?'

'No, just one man in overall charge.' The marketing manager picked up the letter that accompanied the folio and handed it to her, pointing to the director's name.

Zara looked and the room seemed suddenly to zoom about her head, to sway and pitch like a fairground ride. Only the name stayed in focus, the words screaming out at her from the paper. 'Heath Masterson, Managing Director'. Heath Masterson! It couldn't be right. It must be someone else. But how could there be two men with such a distinctive name, and both in advertising? She gasped aloud and caught hold of the edge of the desk, her knuckles showing white as she tried to make the room stay still.

'Zara! Are you all right? Here, sit down.' Pushing her into her chair, Colin ran to get her a glass of water, calling out to Mac as he did so.

But by the time Mac came running in in alarm, Zara had recovered sufficiently to sit up straight and thrust her trembling hands under the desk. 'Sorry. Felt dizzy for a minute. I'm all right now,' she insisted, her voice growing stronger.

'You don't look it. You look as if you've seen a ghost,' Mac told her. 'What's that—water? I think a brandy would be better.'

They fussed over her with the best of intentions, worried frowns on their faces, but all Zara wanted was to be left alone. '*Please.* I've said I'm all right now. No, I don't need to see a doctor. I forgot to have any breakfast, that's all.'

'Then I'll walk you round to the nearest restaurant and make sure that you have a decent lunch,' Colin declared.

'You've been working too hard,' Mac informed her. 'You need a holiday. I can't remember the last time you took one.'

'Oh, for heaven's sake! All this fuss just because I felt giddy for a moment. I'm okay, I tell you. But if it makes you happy I will go and have something to eat. But alone, if you don't mind. I don't need a nursemaid.'

'Huh! If you ask me, that's just what you do need,' Mac told her roundly. 'I'm sure you don't bother to eat or look after yourself properly.'

Zara somehow forced herself to laugh. 'Nonsense! I'm shockingly healthy.' She stood up on legs that felt too weak to hold her and managed to pick up her bag and walk to the door.

'What shall I do about those Masterad ideas?' Colin asked her.

With her hand gripping the door knob, Zara was seized with a sudden wave of hatred. 'Burn them,' she said fiercely. 'Tear them into pieces and burn them!' Then she hastily strode out of the room, leaving the two men staring after her.

She didn't keep her promise to eat, and it was too cold to walk in any of the London parks, so instead Zara hurried through the damp and windy streets until she came to the National Gallery. Here she went inside and sat on a leather seat in one of the huge rooms, staring blindly at a large portrait on the wall while trying desperately to come to terms with the fact that Heath was back in London and probably had been for some time. In one way she supposed she had been lucky; she could so easily have told her marketing manager to set up a meeting with Masterads without bothering to ask the name of the managing director. And then she might have walked unsuspectingly into a room and come face to face with Heath. Her heart froze at the thought. It had been bad enough just seeing his name again, it had brought back so many memories, memories of rejection and humiliation, of hurt and hatred.

Her mind centred on that last thought. God, how she hated the swine! Even now. Even now . . . Zara's hands

tightened into white-knuckled fists in her lap. If only
she could hurt him as he had hurt her. But then she
gave an inward laugh of bitter irony; the man
probably wouldn't even remember her. After all, it
had only lasted a few weeks, and it had been so long
ago. Heath had more than likely forgotten her by the
time he had arrived in America, relieved that he had
got away in time from a situation that might have
turned nasty. Obviously all he had wanted was an
affair, while she had offered him love, herself, her
hopes and ambitions, everything. But he hadn't even
bothered to say goodbye.

Didn't want to risk an hysterical scene, most likely,
Zara thought, trying to drown the pain in cynicism.
But she couldn't help wondering about him, wondering if he had changed, if she would recognise him. All
she had was one tiny photograph of him, taken in a
passport photo booth when they had been waiting for a
train one night and had a few minutes to kill. But she
had always kept it; even after he had dropped her so
cruelly she had been unable to destroy the photo,
keeping it hidden away so that Christopher could
never find it. But even without it Zara knew that she
would always know him, that his features were etched
for ever on her brain and memory.

She wondered, too, if he was married. He probably
was, to some American girl with long legs, big boobs
and a brain, someone who was a perfect hostess and a
tremendous support in his career, Zara decided with
resentful jealousy. Perhaps he even had children. Her
heart caught, seemed to swell with pain. She would

have so loved to have his chilldren, to have this closest of all ties.

People walked and talked around her, looking at the pictures as they passed a wet lunch hour, but Zara was totally unaware of them or of the huge portrait of a cardinal in his red robes in front of her. She was glad that she had found out in time. It would have been terrible if she had agreed to do business with Heath and had to face him. But despite herself she felt an overpowering longing to see him again, to find out whether he did in fact remember her. And she would very much like to grind his face into the dust, of course, that too.

She came back to reality for a moment, her eyes focusing on a black speck on the skirt of the cardinal's robe on the painting. It bothered her, that black speck. Getting up she went to have a closer look and saw that it was a big black fly, but even as she lifted her hand to brush it off she realised that it was part of the picture, that the artist had played a trick that would amuse people long after he and his sitter were dead and gone. It helped to put things back in perspective, that silly little fly. Zara smiled and straightened up. She too had a brain and knew how to use it. And maybe she would give some thought to making Heath smart a little for behaving so badly to her.

The smile widened but it didn't reach her eyes as Zara began to walk out of the gallery and back to her office. She realised that now *she* was in the position of power and that it might be very amusing, not to say satisfying, to woo Heath with the lure of handling *all* her company's advertising, now and in the future, to keep him dangling, and then drop him just as he had dropped her.

Mac was waiting for her in the office and looked up at her anxiously when she strode in. 'Are you feeling better?'

'What?' For a second it didn't register, but then her face cleared. 'Yes, of course. Get me Colin Royle on the intercom, will you?' And when the phone rang in her office Zara picked up the receiver and said, 'Have you—er—got rid of that folio from Masterads? Oh, good. No, you're right, I didn't mean it. In fact I think you can let them know that we might be interested. But nothing definite, you understand. Let them know about the other two agencies we've approached. Yes, I want to know if they'd be willing to really put themselves out for us.'

'What if they suggest a meeting to discuss it?' asked Colin. 'Do I say yes?'

Zara paused for a moment, then took a deep breath. 'Yes. But make it a business lunch, something like that; I don't want a long meeting. Oh, and just say that you'll be bringing one of the directors, don't say which one.'

Colin said he would get on to it right away, slightly surprised, but happy to do her bidding as it coincided with his own ideas.

Zara sat back in her chair, her heart beating too fast as she realised that there was no going back now. Then she began to plan.

As she had expected, Masterads were very keen to get the Panache contract and suggested an early date for a meeting. Zara agreed it, but then cancelled at the last moment and played them around a little before settling for another date. By that time they had received outline ideas from the two better-known and longer-established agencies. Their ideas were good too, very good, but they lacked the almost audacious originality that Masterads had come up with. But it helped to know the terms and ideas of the other agencies when Zara finally arrived for that lunchtime meeting.

It was in London, of course, at one of the very old coffee-houses that had become a restaurant. A place where businessmen had met for centuries to trade and deal, and whose original members had helped to found the London Stock Exchange. It had panelled walls dark with age, narrow twisting wooden staircases, big bow windows overlooking the street, and the tables sectioned off to ensure complete privacy.

Zara had arranged to meet Colin Royle there, but she was deliberately late, which was totally unlike her. She had taken a lot of trouble with her clothes and looked, she knew, quite sensational, in a loose, pure white coat, high-heeled black boots, and a small tricorn hat at a jaunty angle on her upswept hair. There was a small bar opening off the main entrance. Someone opened the door for her and Zara paused in the doorway, looking round, for effect as well as to give her a chance to control her features. Colin was standing at the bar talking to two men who had their backs to her. As he saw her, Colin straightened up and the two men turned round to look, as did several other men in the room.

Heath hadn't known it was her he was to meet, but

he recognised her all right. His eyes widened with interest as he saw her, but then he gave a slight frown which turned to stunned surprise as recognition came. For a moment he stood perfectly still as if he were frozen to the ground. Zara, however, made sure that no sign of recognition or any other emotion showed on her face as she walked forward and smiled at Colin. 'So sorry I'm late—a last-minute phone call that just had to be dealt with.' She turned an innocently smiling face towards his companions. 'Do forgive me—I'm not usually this unpunctual.'

'Of course.' The man with Heath looked towards him, but Heath was still gazing at her as if he couldn't quite believe it.

'May I introduce our managing director, Zara Layston,' Colin said quickly to break the awkward little silence. 'Zara, this is Heath Masterson and Eric Jennings of Masterads.'

'How do you do.' Zara held out a gloved hand first to Eric and then to Heath.

Slowly, Heath took her hand, but held it rather than shook it. 'How do you do—but I'm quite sure we've met before.'

Zara raised a cool, arched brow. 'Really? Were you with some other advertising agency that we've done business with? I'm afraid I don't recall . . .'

'No. We met—socially. Quite some time ago.'

'You must remind me of it some time,' she answered dismissively, removing her hand from his and putting it into her pocket so that no one would notice how unsteady it was.

They went upstairs to the dining-room almost at

once, Zara handing her coat to a waiter and revealing a crisp black and white suit underneath. She was ushered into her seat and Heath slid in opposite her, but the table was wide enough for them not to touch. Colin sat next to Zara and Eric opposite him, and for a while the talk was general as they chose what they wanted to eat, knowing that whichever of the traditional dishes they chose would be superbly cooked and presented.

When they had ordered, Heath looked at her and said, 'You seem to have come a long way since last we met.'

'Have I?' Zara tried to keep her voice light, to hide the crazy swell of emotions that raged behind her coolness. He had changed so little, hardly looked any older at all. There was no grey in his hair, it was still dark and thick, and no lines on his face, except perhaps round his mouth, and those were more the twists of cynicism or mockery than age. He was thirty-five, in his prime now, she supposed, and as devastating as ever. Yes, she would have known him anywhere, because this was the man she had loved, the man who had tossed her aside like a boring book. 'You said we met socially, I think?'

'Yes, at a party. It must be—seven years ago now. Yes, that's right.'

'Good heavens!' Zara gave a little trill of laughter, 'What an astonishing memory you must have, Mr Masterson. I can hardly remember people I met at a party last week, let alone that long ago.' Deliberately changing the subject, she said, 'Colin tells me that your agency is comparatively new?'

Heath's dark eyes settled on her speculatively for a moment before he replied. 'Yes, that's right. I had been working in the States, but I came back to London two years ago and started the company.'

'You didn't take over an existing one and change the name?'

'No. I preferred to start from scratch and recruit my own staff.'

'You must find England quite a change after America. What made you decide to come back?'

Heath shrugged and gave a slightly twisted smile, an action Zara remembered so well that her heart lurched and she didn't hear what he was saying for several minutes. She came back to reality to find him looking at her rather quizzically and realised that he had asked her a question, but she was saved from having to ask him to repeat it by the arrival of the waiter with their first course. Heath went to pour her some wine, but she put her hand over the glass. 'No, thanks, I prefer water.'

'Do you? Or do you just prefer to keep a clear head when discussing business?'

'That too,' Zara admitted. 'And I have a lot of work to get through this afternoon.'

'You must have already worked very hard to be the managing director of such a successful company at such a comparatively early age,' Heath complimented her. 'You can still only be—what—twenty-five, I think?'

His knowing her age surprised her, but she said coolly, 'I simply worked my way up the firm, that's all.'

But Colin had heard and put in with a smile, 'That is

definitely an understatement. Zara *is* Panache. Or rather Webster & Layston.'

Heath looked across at her ringless hands. 'The name Layston surprises me. I had heard that you were married.'

'Really?' Aside from wondering how on earth he knew, Zara was acutely conscious of Colin listening with pricked ears beside her. She had dropped her married name on the day that she and Christopher were divorced as she felt that she had no right to it, and gradually, because of staff changes in the company, there was no one in the head office who knew she had been married at all. That there was great curiosity among her colleagues about her social/love life, she was fully aware, and it looked as if Colin was going to have some juicy titbits to take back to them. 'Yes, I was,' she admitted reluctantly. 'But it broke up some time ago.'

'And your sister? I'm afraid I've forgotten her name.'

Zara looked at him antagonistically. 'But you seem to have a fantastic memory, Mr Masterson . . .'

'Heath,' he broke in.

But she ignored him. 'My sister is fine, thank you. She's married to a doctor and has two children. Is that how we met? Were you a friend of Denise?'

She looked at him in bland enquiry and Heath's eyes settled intently on her face. 'No.' He shook his head a little. 'I was never a friend of *your sister*.'

He stressed the last two words a little, but Zara ignored that too. Quickly she brought the conversation back to business and kept it there. She had to admit that Heath knew his stuff; he had an answer to every query that she raised about the outlines he had given them for the Game, Set and Match promotion. Sometimes he deferred to Eric Jennings, but Zara could tell that this was from a good relations point of view, not because he didn't know the answer himself. She had gone into his suggestions thoroughly, looking for flaws, but had found very few and these mostly through lack of knowledge of each individual Panache shop. And when she pointed out impracticalities Heath agreed readily enough, not attempting to bluster or make any excuses.

They had reached the coffee stage, Zara refusing a pudding, and she reached out to pick up the cream just as Heath went to hand it to her. Their hands collided. Heath apologised as Zara jerked away, unable to bear any physical contact with him. His eyes went swiftly to her face, for a second open and vulnerable, but then the mask closed down and she was her cool, efficient self again.

Colin and Eric were talking animatedly and hadn't noticed anything. Heath glanced at them and then leaned forward, one elbow on the table as he stirred his coffee. 'You know,' he said softly so that only she could hear, 'I think you do remember me after all.'

But Zara shook her head decisively. 'I'm afraid not.'

'In that case,' he went on smoothly, 'why don't you have dinner with me one evening soon so that I can remind you of where we met—and how well we knew one another?'

Zara gave a disparaging laugh. 'Is this how you usually do business, Mr Masterson?'

'This isn't business. This is—personal.'

The way he looked at her when he said it brought so many bittersweet memories flooding back. Zara's hands tightened in her lap, but she managed to keep all emotion out of her face except a slight disdain. 'Sorry, no.'

Heath's left eyebrow rose quizzically. 'Afraid, Zara?'

She returned his look levelly. 'Of what?'

'Of the past. Of remembering.'

She gave a delighted laugh that made Colin and Eric turn to look at her. 'How mysterious you are, Mr Masterson! Maybe I will let you tell me some time. But right now I have to get back to work. Thank you so much for lunch—it was delicious.' She got to her feet and they all moved out into the entrance area. 'It's been an interesting talk, Mr Masterson, and Colin and I will certainly give a lot of thought to your proposals, but we must also listen to the agencies we've used before.'

The waiter brought her coat and went to hold it for her, but Heath took it from him, lifting it on to her shoulders and holding his hands there for a moment until she stepped away. After putting on her gloves she held out her hand to him again. 'Goodbye, it was nice to meet you. But perhaps I should add "again" as you seem so sure that we've met.' She turned to say goodbye to his assistant, pleased that an uncertain look was back in Heath's eyes. On the whole, Zara thought, as she and Colin took a taxi back to the office, she had done rather well. She had been so afraid that she would betray her real feelings when she saw him, but she had made just that one small slip. She remembered how quickly he had picked it up, and how quickly, too, he had recognised her. At least she had made a lasting impression on him, if nothing else, Zara thought bitterly.

Colin said something to her and she gave him a vague look. 'What?'

'I said what did you think of Heath Masterson?'

'Oh, okay. What did you?'

'I thought he was extremely efficient, and full of good ideas. I'm a hundred per cent behind us giving them the contract,' he said enthusiastically. 'I think it's the kind of campaign that will really make our rivals sit up and take notice.'

'Are you indeed?' Zara answered drily. 'I'd rather our *customers* took notice and came in and bought.'

Colin grinned, having had enough wine to make him cheeky. 'You know what I mean. When shall I draw up the contract with Masterads?'

For a moment Zara looked unseeingly out of the window before turning to him again. 'You won't,' she said shortly. 'I have no intention of giving them the contract.'

He looked at her in astonishment. 'But why? Their ideas are first class. Is it the terms or something that's put you off? Because if so I can probably negotiate...'

'No, it isn't that. I just don't want to do business with them, that's all.'

He gave her a shrewd look. 'Because Masterson said he'd met you before?'

'Because he *claimed* that he'd met me before. I don't remember him,' Zara lied.

'But he seemed to know things about you.'

'A couple of facts, that's all. Things that anyone could have found out if they'd wanted to make that kind of claim. Perhaps he thought a previous acquaintance might influence me in their favour. But it's had the opposite effect.'

'All right,' Colin said resignedly. 'You're the boss, but I still think their campaign would have been the most effective. I'll write to Masterson tomorrow and tell him we've chosen one of the other agencies.'

'No, not tomorrow. Let them go on hoping for a while longer. I'll tell you when.'

He frowned. 'This doesn't sound like you at all, Zara. Masterads must have put a lot of work into this already, and could be holding back some of their key workers for the campaign. They might even turn down other work in the hope of getting the contract.'

'Then that's a risk they have to take,' Zara said brutally as the taxi drew up outside their office building. 'Just do as I ask, please, Colin.'

Going into her office, she told Mac that she didn't want to be disturbed for an hour and settled down at her desk with a sheaf of papers in front of her, but she had only been looking through them for about five minutes when she gave up all pretence and sat with her chin resting on her hands, thinking of Heath. She still didn't know if he was married; he wore only one ring on his right hand, but he had worn that when she had known him; it was a present from his parents for his twenty-first birthday. But she did know that he had lost none of his charm and the magnetism that had so attracted her in the beginning. Perhaps, now that he was his own master, he had a slightly more arrogant air, as if he was used to giving orders, but he still had that lazy smile that did crazy things to her insides. And which somehow made her hate him all the more. He uses his charm deliberately, she thought bitterly. To entice girls—and now to try and win the Panache contract. My God, did he really think I'd succumb to his charms and go out to dinner with him if I'd remembered him? After the way he walked out on me? The man's mad! Or else so sure of his effect on women that he thought I'd come running back for more of the same.

Pushing her chair violently back, she stood up and glared angrily at the innocent wall, her face bleak, her green eyes cold as glacial ice. She was *glad* she had seen him. Because now she would have no qualms whatsoever about doing him as much harm as she possibly could.

CHAPTER THREE

MASTERADS, or rather Heath, was very patient; he waited almost a week before getting Eric Jennings to phone Colin to ask if they had come to a decision over the advertising contract. Colin in turn rang Zara and asked the same question.

'Tell him no,' she replied baldly.

'I can't keep them dangling much longer,' Colin complained. 'They're going to demand an answer one way or another soon.'

'So when they do let me know,' she told him.

Later that afternoon her phone rang again and Mac said there was a personal call for her.

'Who is it?'

'It's Heath Masterson of Masterads.'

'I'd hardly call that a personal call.'

'He insists that it's not about business.'

'Does he indeed? Tell him I'm not available,' Zara instructed with some satisfaction. So Heath was starting to panic, was he? Good. Well, he could sweat a bit longer before she gave him the bad news.

She was going out to dinner that evening, having received a rather unexpected invitation to the home of a middle-aged couple, Sir John and Lady Ward, whom Zara had met at a conference on Youth Employment in the Clothing Industry recently. Sir John was in the Civil Service and his wife had taken an active part as hostess at the conference. Zara hadn't been invited to bring an escort so guessed, rather wryly, that she had been asked to make the numbers up, especially as Lady Ward had only phoned the invitation through a couple of days ago. But she didn't really mind; it was always stimulating to meet new people and sometimes, if she met someone really interesting, having an escort could cramp her style.

So that evening Zara put on a green evening dress that exactly matched the colour of her eyes, and took a taxi to the Kensington address that she had been given. It turned out to be a house set in a terrace in a side road off Kensington High Street, a pretty Georgian town house with an authentic bow window on the first floor overlooking the street. It was to this room that Zara was directed after she had handed the maid her coat. Her host and hostess greeted her at the door and then Lady Ward began to introduce her to the people who had already arrived. It was to be quite a large dinner party, evidently; there were already about eight people there besides the Wards, all married couples, two of whom Zara knew slightly and began to chat with. She wondered rather cynically who had been invited for her—or vice versa—but she wasn't kept in suspense very long; after about five minutes the last guest arrived and Lady Ward moved over to the door to greet him. Zara had her back to the door but took a casual step sideways so that she could glance across and see what the man was like. She took that one glance and then swiftly looked away, her heart jumping in her chest, colour flooding from her cheeks. The other unaccompanied guest was Heath! Wearing a similar black evening suit to the one he had worn on the night she had met him. Seeing him so unexpectedly sent her senses reeling with shock, unable to hear a word that anyone said to her, and her hand holding the glass of sherry shaking uncontrollably.

'Careful, you'll spill your drink!' a woman exclaimed, and somehow she managed to give a thin-lipped smile and bring herself back under control.

By the time Lady Ward had introduced Heath to the other people in the room and reached her group, Zara had subdued her emotions, her numb brain having already recovered enough to figure out just why she had been invited—so that Heath could work on her for the Panache contract! A surge of anger flamed through her veins; she hated being used like this. So it was a very frosty acknowledgement that Heath received when Lady Ward brought him over. She merely nodded to Heath's, 'Well, hallo again,' and made no attempt to transfer her drink to her left hand so that she could shake hands with him as the other guests did.

Turning back to the woman she had been talking to before he arrived, Zara said, 'You were telling me about your holiday,' and the woman happily picked up where she had left off. An amused look came into Heath's eyes, but he began to chat easily with the other three people in the group. Zara didn't look at him, apparently giving all her attention to the person she was talking to, but she was very aware of Heath, the memories of that first time she had met him strong in her mind. Somehow his presence filled the room, dwarfing the other men there, emasculating them by his height and casual self-assurance. That he had lost none of his attraction was obvious; every woman in the room had perked up a little when he had come in, was standing a little straighter and talking just a tone higher to try and attract his attention. Even the woman Zara was talking to kept giving him surreptitious glances and soon turned to join in the other conversation.

'Shall we go in to dinner?' Lady Ward's raised voice broke through the chatter and the husbands and wives naturally paired up, leaving Zara and Heath to go in together at the end.

Zara turned to put her glass on a convenient table and didn't look at Heath as he stood aside to let her go ahead of him through the door. As she had guessed, they were seated next to each other around the middle of the long table. After pulling her chair out for her, Heath sat down on her right. 'What a pleasant surprise to meet you again so soon,' he said smoothly.

Zara raised a very cold eyebrow. 'Surprise?' she asked, expecting him to say that he hadn't known she was to be there.

But he smiled disarmingly and said, 'Well, not a surprise for me, I must admit; Evelyn had already told me that you'd been invited. As a matter of fact I tried to phone you at your office to ask if I could give you a lift here tonight—but you weren't available.'

He paused before the last few words and raised his eyebrows as if he hadn't believed it, but Zara took no notice. He was very smooth, she thought, and very clever to have admitted that he knew she would be here. 'You must know Lady Ward well if you call her by her first name,' she remarked.

'Very well. Both her and Sir John. They're old friends of my own parents.'

'And as such are probably very willing to do you a favour when you ask it?' Zara guessed, her anger increasing.

Heath looked amused, as if he already knew what was coming. 'Yes. And you're quite right, I did ask them to invite you tonight. I wanted to meet you again on neutral ground and . . .'

But Zara interrupted him, her green eyes flashing angry fire. 'I shall tell you this just once—I don't mix business with pleasure—if that's what this dinner is supposed to be. And if you mention business even once I warn you I shall scream. Very loudly! And then I shall leave—and let the people here draw what conclusions they like from it.'

She didn't know quite how he would react to that, but she certainly didn't expect to see a raptly admiring look in his eyes and for him to shake his head and say, 'Ah, now I certainly don't remember that!'

'Remember what?'

'Your ever being angry before. I should certainly have remembered if you had. It—leaves a lasting impression. But when I knew you it wasn't anger that—you *said*—you felt.'

Zara looked at him speechlessly for a moment, wishing she could say a whole lot of things about that, but as she couldn't, she turned her back on him to talk to her other neighbour, remembering belatedly to eat some of the starter in front of her.

She talked to the other man exclusively through the fish course until his wife claimed his attention, and to the people opposite while the main course was being served. But then Heath joined in that conversation until somehow she found that everyone else had turned away and she was left with no one but him to talk to.

For the life of her she couldn't think of anything to say. Heath looked at her set profile, gave a small smile and said, 'This is excellent beef, isn't it?'

'Yes, delicious,' Zara agreed mechanically, then looked at him quickly as he laughed.

'It's pheasant,' he pointed out with a grin.

'Oh! Is it? Yes, of course.' She realised that she hadn't the slightest idea what she had been eating.

'I'm sorry if I've made you angry,' Heath said softly. 'Please don't blame Evelyn; she did as I asked with the best of intentions.'

Zara glanced at their hostess at the head of the table, then back at Heath. 'Did she have any choice?'

He smiled. 'Not a lot. It took me quite some time to find someone who knew you, and I was very persuasive.'

'I can imagine,' she said drily. 'Just as I can imagine just why you wanted to see me.'

'Can you?' Heath looked at her contemplatively. 'I wonder if you really do or if you're just pretending.'

'I don't—pretend.'

'Don't you?' he said enigmatically. But then with a swift change of mood, 'Believe me, I didn't want to see you to discuss business. I don't like taking my work home with me any more than you do. But I wanted us to meet socially so that maybe we could start renewing our acquaintance.'

'I don't remember any acquaintance to renew,' Zara answered shortly.

'Tut, tut, tut,' he mocked. 'And who was it said she didn't pretend?'

A slight flush coloured Zara's cheeks but she wouldn't admit that he was right. She pushed her plate away, unable to eat. 'Even if we had met before, I make it a rule not to become friendly with anyone I do business with, either customers or people we buy from. There's too much cut and thrust in business to let friendship stand in the way. So I'm afraid I don't subscribe to the old-pals act, Mr Masterson.'

'In that case you must lead a very lonely life, Zara. Which is a great shame.'

'On the contrary,' she retorted. 'My social life is fine, thank you very much.' Her voice had risen a little and she became aware that one or two people were looking at them, so she quickly smiled across the table and started a new conversation.

The meal seemed to go on interminably with a pudding and then cheese and biscuits before everyone could get up and move back into the drawing-room for coffee. Sir John came over and started chatting to her about the progress made after the conference and to thank her for a youth training course in textile design that her company was sponsoring.

'I took a similar course at night school,' Zara told him, 'and it was very helpful.'

He looked surprised. 'I thought for sure you must have taken a degree at college.'

'No, I never went to college.' Zara became aware of someone coming over to her with a glass of brandy as she spoke and half-turned to see Heath at her elbow.

He gave her rather a strange look and took Sir John's place as he went on to speak to others of his guests. 'You didn't go to university?' Zara shook her head. 'Fail your A-levels or something?'

'No, I didn't choose to go.'

He frowned. 'But I thought . . .' Then he gave a rather angry shake of his head. 'It hardly matters now. So how *did* you come to be head of Webster & Layston—by taking evening-class courses?' he asked incredulously.

Deciding this didn't come under the heading of business so she needn't scream, Zara answered, 'Mostly. But Mr Webster taught me a great deal.'

'And where is Mr Webster now? Did you buy him out?' Heath asked with an edge of sarcasm in his tone that Zara didn't like.

Her chin came up. 'No. As a matter of fact he retired. He got marri . . .' She broke of as some of the guests raised their voices, asking their host to play the piano for them, and after a little more persuasion he moved across to the baby grand in one corner of the large room. My God, Zara thought, I've come to an amateur talent night!

Beside her she heard Heath laugh. 'You should see your face,' he whispered in her ear.

Zara hastily schooled her features but gave him a dark look under her lashes as she sat down in the chair he pulled forward for her, bringing another forward so that he could sit down next to her. She quite expected to be bored out of her mind listening to an amateur trying to play classical music for the next hour, and

wondered how soon she could decently make her
excuses and escape. Her heart sank as Sir John played a
few bars of very sombre music, his face solemn, but
then he gave a big grin and broke into jazz. He was
good, too, playing like a professional and improvising
as he went along.

With an inward sigh of relief, Zara relaxed in her
chair, her foot beginning to tap in time with the music.
She had always loved jazz, but it was ages since she had
listened to any. When any of the men she knew took
her to a concert it always seemed to be to classical
music, which she liked well enough, but jazz made her
feel young again. A sad look came into Zara's face;
sometimes, at the most stupid moments, she felt deep
regret for the youth she had lost, a youth that had
ended so abruptly when Heath had ditched her and she
had married Christopher. From then on it had been all
work, there hadn't been any play at all, and even now,
when she was taken out to concerts and night clubs, she
didn't always enjoy herself; more often than not her
thoughts would return to ideas and plans she had for
Panache, thoughts that she ought to have left behind
her at the office but never could.

Heath moved beside her, making her remember that
he was to blame for the change in her life that had so
ruined her youth, and she shot him a look of such
venomous hatred that his eyes widened in shocked
astonishment. But the next instant Zara had looked
away, her features under control again.

Sir John went on playing for about half an hour, but
she was too conscious of Heath sitting beside her to
enjoy it any more. As soon as he stopped, refusing to

play any longer, Zara stood up to take her leave, as did two other couples. Her thanks to Sir John and Lady Ward were rather stilted—how could they be otherwise when she knew that she had only been invited at Heath's request? Lady Ward came downstairs with them and while the maid was fetching her coat Zara asked if she could use the phone to call a taxi.

But Heath had followed them down the stairs and said, 'No need for a taxi, I have my car outside.'

'Thank you, but I wouldn't dream of troubling you,' Zara said coldly.

'It's no trouble at all. It would be a pleasure.'

She shot him an angry glance. 'I don't want to take you out of your way.'

Heath's lips twitched. 'You don't know which is my way,' he pointed out softly.

'Nor you mine,' she shot back at him.

'Please, I insist,' he said, raising his voice again, and Zara realised that to go on arguing in the hallway like this was making them look ridiculous. So she had to nod resentfully and let him help her on with her coat. His car, a Mercedes sports saloon, was parked a short way down the road. The pavements were icy, but Heath made no attempt to hold her arm, sensing that she would reject any help, but he held the door for her as she angrily got in.

'Where to?' he asked, getting in beside her.

'Chelsea,' she snapped.

It didn't take long to pull up outside her building. Zara said, 'Thanks,' and made to get out, but Heath caught her wrist.

'Why are you so mad at me?' he demanded.

'I should have thought that was obvious. I don't like being—manipulated. Being asked out to dinner under false pretences.'

'I suggested we have dinner together myself, but you just ignored me. How else was I to get to see you?'

'Maybe the fact that I ignored your invitation should have told you that I wasn't interested in seeing you again,' Zara retorted.

'Why not? Just what is it you think you've got against me, Zara?'

She stared at him speechlessly for a moment, then bit back the angry words of hatred and said shortly, 'I told you; I make a point of not having any social connections with people I do business with.'

Again she tried to get out of the car, but Heath still held her wrist, and he also was becoming angry now. 'But you have no intention of giving my agency your contract, have you?' he demanded brusquely.

True to her threat, Zara opened her mouth and began to scream, but he quickly put his hand over it to silence her. His angry dark eyes glared down into hers for a moment, then he gave a muttered curse and replaced his hand by his mouth.

Surprise held Zara rigid for a few seconds, but then a flame of fury fiercer than any emotion she had ever known seared through her and she tried to jerk her head away. But Heath had put a hand behind her neck and was holding her captive to his mouth. She tried to struggle and push him away, hitting out at him with a strength grown out of anger and outrage. Her fist connected with the side of his face and he gave a grunt of annoyance against her mouth, but then his arms went round her, crushing her to him so that she couldn't struggle any more, could only hold herself in rigid fury as his kiss deepened. The hard insidiousness of his lips began to get to her and in desperation Zara tried to bite him, but he bent her head back and forced her to open her mouth beneath his, his greater strength dominating her into a rebellious surrender that made her hate him all the more.

His lips ravaged hers in unhurried violation, exploring at their will, bringing back memories from the past that she could never forget, no matter how hard she tried. And it seemed that this was just what Heath intended, for when he finally raised his head he said roughly, '*Now* do you remember me?'

Zara stared at him in the dim light of the car, her breath ragged with anger and hate. 'Yes,' she said fiercely, 'I remember you. How could I do otherwise? You haven't changed a bit!'

'Then why pretend you didn't know me?'

But she wasn't going to be drawn into that argument. If he hadn't kissed her she would never have admitted it. 'I'm going in,' she told him forcefully. 'And if you try to stop me I'll—I'll . . .'

'Do what? Try to scream again?' Heath's hand went to her neck to remind her of what had happened the last time.

'Take your rotten hands off me!' she spat at him.

He stared at her, slowly lowering his hand. 'Zara, I don't understand. Why are you . . .?'

'Don't you? Then maybe your memory isn't so good after all.' Quickly she got out of the car, immune to the icy wind that blew her hair around her head, and slammed the door, then turned and ran into the entrance to her building, her furious hands fumbling for the key. Behind her she heard Heath's door slam and turned to see him coming after her, tall and menacing in his dark overcoat.

'Zara, this is crazy,' be began. 'Why are you . . .?'

But in panic she had pushed the door bell and the night porter came quickly to open it, looking at her in surprise. 'Forget your key?'

'No. I . . . My hands were so cold.'

She walked quickly inside, but the doorman barred the way to Heath. 'Is this gentleman with you, Miss Layston?'

Heath opened his mouth to speak, but Zara said hurriedly, 'No, he isn't. Please don't let him in.' Then she gave Heath one last look of scorching dislike before turning on her heel and running up the stairs to her flat, too angry to even wait for the lift.

Once inside the haven of her own home, she locked and bolted the door as if shutting out his physical presence could shut Heath out of her thoughts. But it couldn't of course, nothing could do that. She slumped down into a chair, still angry at the humiliating way he had kissed her. How dared he? Did he still think she was some little schoolgirl he could win over by that rough, masterful approach? If he thought for one minute that . . . Her thoughts broke suddenly and she put her hands up to her face. Oh God, how she had longed for his kisses when he went away. She would have given anything, anything! for him to have held her again, even as forcefully as he had tonight. Whenever Christopher had kissed her in the following

years she had wished it was Heath, she just couldn't
help herself. So she had tried to avoid his kisses, but he
had forced her to submit and so had seen the truth in
her eyes. Then anger and jealousy had made Christopher cruel, had made him do unspeakable things that
had killed the guilt that kept her as his wife.

Other men, kind men, good-looking men, had kissed
her since and Zara had enjoyed it to a degree, because
it was pleasant to be desired, to be admired, but no
man's kisses had ever had the same effect on her. None
had sent her senses whirling with desire, had created an
electric spark that made her come alive when he
touched her, had set her heart on fire with anticipation
and excitement. Even though at times, when she was
driven to desperation by frustration, she had deliberately tried to find such a man, there had been no one.
Often she didn't even need to kiss a man to know that it
wasn't any good, and now she had learned to live with
frustration, to conquer it and channel her energies into
her work.

But now Heath had come back into her life and with
one kiss melted the thick wall of ice she had built to
protect her buried emotions.

Zara sat in the chair for a long time, trying to regain
her poise, trying to rebuild her shattered defences, but
in the end she had to admit to herself that nothing was
going to be the same again. But above all other
emotions there was hatred for Heath, that and the
fierce need to hurt him as he had hurt her. Getting up,
Zara began to pace about the room, thinking. Not
giving Heath the Panache contract would be a blow to
him, but a very small one that he could ride with ease.

It was hardly the hurt that she had in mind. She wanted to deal him a blow that he would remember always, from which it would take him a very long time to recover, if he recovered at all.

Putting her trained mind to work on the problem, she went over to her desk and made a few notes, the tension in her face slowly relaxing as she began to see what she could do.

The next morning Mac was given some orders that made him raise his eyebrows. 'You want me to find out about Masterson's personal life as well as how his business is doing?' he asked in surprise.

'That's what I said,' Zara answered crisply.

Her secretary gave her a searching look. 'That's going a bit far, isn't it? I mean, it's all very well to find out whether a firm you intend to do business with is solvent, but to pry into the boss's private life is . . .'

'Mac,' Zara broke in, her tone a warning, 'just see to it, will you?'

He gave her a long, speculative look, wondering what she was up to, but knew that there was no arguing with her when she had that determined thrust to her chin. 'Okay, I'll put the investigation agency on to him.'

'Good. And tell Colin Royle I want to see him, will you, please?'

Colin was in her office within five minutes. 'Made up your mind which of the agencies you're going to use for the Game, Set and Match promotion?' he asked at once, putting two big folios on her desk.

'Yes. I'm going to use Masterads after all.'

He stared at her in astounded surprise. 'But—but

you said you didn't want them!'

'I know what I said, but now I've changed my mind,' Zara replied offhandedly.

'But you never change your mind once you've made it up! Why, that's—that's downright *feminine*!'

Despite herself, Zara couldn't help smiling at the consternation in his face. 'I'm very sorry,' she said contritely. 'But you did recommend the Masterad outline, didn't you?'

'Why yes, but . . .'

'So I've decided to follow your advice. You can phone them and tell them we've decided to give them the contract. Then you'd better get together with them and work out the final details as soon as possible. Keep me informed at every stage, won't you?'

Colin gave her a puzzled, slightly suspicious look. 'Yes, of course. But don't you want to be in on planning the campaign? You usually do.'

Zara shook her head. 'I'm quite sure you're capable of handling it. Just let me know what you've decided, all the details.'

Colin shrugged, but nodded, realising that having to report back to Zara all the time was going to mean twice as much work for him. He wondered what had got into her; she seemed to be acting completely out of character over this Masterads business.

When he had gone Zara sat back in her chair, satisfied with what she had set in hand. It would extend Heath's company quite a bit to undertake this contract, but would give him the confidence to extend himself even more when she dangled the contract to advertise her expansion into household goods under his nose. She was, in fact, setting a sprat to catch a mackerel. When Heath fell she wanted him to land with such an almighty thud that he would never get up again. That giving him the contract would probably bring her into Heath's company again was the price she would just have to pay to gain his ultimate downfall.

The first she heard from him was a letter acknowledging the terms of the contract and thanking her for giving it to his agency. The usual things. But what wasn't so usual was the basket of yellow roses he sent round to her flat. They arrived on a day when snow was falling and the traffic in central London was completely snarled up. Her taxi had been caught in a jam for so long that in the end Zara had abandoned it and walked home the rest of the way.

'These flowers came for you, Miss Layston,' the porter told her. 'Make a nice bit of colour on such a terrible day, don't they?'

'They certainly do,' Zara agreed, her spirits brightening. But her feelings changed completely when she opened the card and read, 'Thanks for proving me wrong. Won't you waive your principles just once and have dinner with me tonight? Heath.' And below his name was a phone number that she guessed was his home. Her face hardening, she said, 'I hear your wife has the 'flu.'

'Yes,' the porter agreed. 'She's been bad all this last week. Feeling very low, she is.'

Zara smiled at him. 'Well, why don't you give her these roses? Perhaps they'll cheer her up a little.'

'Are you sure, miss? Oh, she'll be right pleased with them. Loves flowers, the missus does.'

Walking away from his continued thanks, Zara
went up to her flat, the card still in her hand, her
thoughts angry. Did Heath really think she was going
to change her mind and go out with him? Surely she
had made it clear that she wanted nothing more to do
with him? But that was before she had given his agency
the contract, she realised. If she had changed her mind
about that then maybe it was right for him to expect
her to change her mind about going out with him, too.
Well, he could think again. Zara tossed his card into
the waste paper basket and went into the bathroom to
shower and change into more casual clothes.

She had no plans for the evening; Richard was due
to fly to the Middle East on business that day, and
although she could quite easily have called any of half
a dozen men to suggest going out to dinner, she didn't
bother, preferring to have an evening at home. After
putting on a pair of cream leather trousers that fitted as
snugly as a glove and a soft sweater over them, Zara
went into the kitchen to fix herself something to eat.
Her housekeeper kept the fridge plentifully supplied,
but when she ate alone Zara preferred to eat simply, an
omelette or a salad or something. Tonight, because it
was so cold outside, she decided on soup and a prawn
omelette with a side salad and had just begun to make it
when the doorphone rang. There was a camera built
into the main entrance with a small screen by her front
door so that Zara could see who was waiting outside.
Switching it on, she was surprised to see Richard's face
looking up at her. 'Come on up,' she exclaimed into the
phone, and waited until he came to her front door.
'Richard! I thought you were on your way to Bahrein?'

'Hallo, darling.' He gave her a warm kiss. 'The airport is snowbound—no flights until tomorrow at least. So I thought I'd come round and spend the evening with you, if that's okay.'

'Of course. Have you eaten? I'm just going to make myself something.'

'All I've had is an airport cafeteria snack. All the passengers were just sitting around for hours waiting for the weather to clear, then we were told it's all off for today. There's nothing I hate more than sitting around waiting. Such a waste of time.'

He had followed Zara into her sitting-room and without asking she went to the drinks tray and poured him a large whisky and soda. 'Here, perhaps this will help.'

'Thanks. You look very attractive—but then you always do—to me.' Slipping an arm round her slim waist, Richard said, 'Lord, Zara, I wish you'd marry me. I just know we could be happy together. Do you know, I was glad when they said the flights were cancelled because it meant that I'd be able to see you tonight.'

Zara smiled at the compliment but refused to be drawn into committing herself. Actually she had been quite relieved to know that Richard was going abroad for three weeks because it gave her some breathing space. She glanced at him as she went back into the kitchen; he had all the attributes that went to make a perfect husband: gentleness, clean-cut looks, success, good manners, he was the kind of man you could always depend on to look after you and cherish you. With him, Zara was sure, she could live a very contented life—if she hadn't met Heath first. But having known love once there was no way she could settle for second best. Not yet at least; maybe one day she would change her mind, but she wasn't ready to accept it yet.

She was busy in the kitchen when the doorphone rang again. 'It's okay, I'll get it,' Richard called. A minute later he put his head round the door and said in a stiff tone, 'It's somebody called Masterson. He said you were expecting him, so I told him to come up.'

'Oh no!' Zara exclaimed in dismay, but it was too late to do anything about it, Heath had already run up the stairs and was pushing open the front door that Richard had left ajar.

'Hallo, Zara,' Heath said cheerfully, his dark eyes assessing the situation. 'I was late getting home and thought I might have missed your phone call, so I came straight over.'

'You didn't miss my phone call because I didn't make one,' Zara answered frostily. Adding, 'As you can see, I'm busy this evening.'

'Yes.' Heath looked at Richard. 'Hallo. I don't think we've met.'

So then she had no choice but to introduce the two men, Richard greeting Heath warily, but Heath completely at ease, as if Richard were the one butting in and not him. To put him in his place, Zara said coldly, 'Richard and I were just about to eat, so if you don't mind . . .'

'Not at all. I'd be delighted to take pot luck,' Heath answered incorrigibly, deliberately misunderstanding her.

Zara gave a little gasp of annoyance, her colour rising. 'That wasn't an invitation,' she told him roundly.

'Wasn't it? That's a shame.' He smiled at her, a smile that caught at her heartstrings and made her catch her breath. 'Are you going to turn me out into the snow, Zara?' he asked softly, his eyes holding hers.

For a moment she couldn't speak, could only gaze into his eyes. It was Richard who broke the silence. He looked from one to the other of them, his face becoming grim with recognition and disappointment, then said, 'I'm the one who must go. I didn't realise . . . I should have phoned first.'

'No!' Zara swung round and caught hold of his sleeve. 'You mustn't go. I won't let you,' she said fiercely. But even as she said it knew that she was only begging him to stay because she didn't want to be left alone with Heath. Trying to lighten her voice, she said, 'Don't be silly, Richard. Our meal is ready.'

'Then I'm obviously in the way,' Heath said easily. He looked round the room for the flowers he had sent, then walked ahead of her down the hallway to the front door, leaving Richard in the sitting-room. 'Perhaps you didn't get my message.'

'Yes, I got it,' Zara replied coldly. 'But I chose to ignore it.'

'I see. And the flowers?'

'The porter's wife,' she told him scornfully.

Heath's eyebrows flickered, but he betrayed no other emotion. 'Lucky lady! Does she get all your flowers—or just mine?'

'Just yours,' she said tauntingly.

He nodded. 'That figures.' He gestured towards the sitting-room. 'Are you and he serious about each other?'

'Mind your own damn business!' Zara snapped back.

Heath grinned. 'I thought not. Will you have dinner with me tomorrow night?'

'No.'

'When, then?'

'Never. I've already told you several times ...'

'Yes, I know what you told me. And I'm beginning to think you're hiding behind your so-called principles, Zara.'

'Why should I do that?'

'Because I think you're afraid of me. Or at least of admitting that you once—liked me.'

Liked him! That was the understatement of the century. But Zara shook her head. 'You're quite wrong. I'm not in the least afraid of you.'

Heath studied her face for a moment, then said, 'Just tell me one thing; why did you give me the Panache contract?'

'Because your agency came up with the best ideas, of course. We liked your approach. Why else would I decide to use you?'

'Ah, why indeed. So you don't let personalities interfere with business?'

'No, certainly not.'

But then he shook her by saying, 'Then why, I wonder, do you let them interfere with pleasure? We could have a good time together, Zara, if only you'd give us another chance.'

Her face hardening, Zara yanked open the door. 'One chance with you is enough to last anyone a lifetime, thank you very much. Good night.'

He gave her a sardonic look. 'Enjoy yourself with the boy-friend—if you can. Goodnight, Zara.' And he turned away just as she angrily shut the door in his face.

CHAPTER FOUR

ZARA's colour was still high as she went back into the sitting-room. 'Sorry about that,' she apologised. 'I'll just set the table, then we can eat. Would you like to open a bottle of wine, Richard?'

He didn't have to be told where she kept the wine; he had eaten at the flat enough times to know, but the grim look was still on Richard's face as they sat down to eat. 'Do you know Masterson well?' he asked abruptly.

Zara's heart sank; the last thing she wanted was a catechism on her relationship with Heath, but she tried to keep her tone light as she said, 'No, not very well at all. He's the managing director of Masterads, the agency we're using to promote our sportswear.'

He looked surprised. 'It didn't look as if you were just business acquaintances.'

'Well, that's all we are,' Zara said with finality.

But Richard was unwise enough not to take the hint. 'But he would obviously like to become more, wouldn't he?' he pursued jealously.

'Possibly he would,' she agreed. 'But I definitely wouldn't. So let's just leave it, shall we?'

'I'm sorry,' he said stiffly. 'I just thought I had the right to know . . .'

'No,' Zara cut in fiercely. 'You don't have any rights as far as I'm concerned. No man does!'

He stared at her in shocked surprise, then put down his soup spoon. 'Well, that really tells me what kind of place I hold in your life. And here was I deluding myself into thinking that you cared about me and might one day soon agree to marry me!'

He went to stand up, but Zara put a hand on his arm. 'I'm sorry, Richard. Of course I care about you. You're one of my closest friends. But—but I don't want to get married again.'

Richard sat slowly back in his chair, his eyes fixed on her face. 'Again?'

'Yes. I've been married before. Oh,' she made a dismissive gesture with her hand, 'it was the usual thing. I was far too young and realised almost at once that it was a mistake. It was all over long ago.'

'But it left you scarred?' Richard said slowly.

'Scarred and scared,' Zara agreed, picking up her spoon and beginning to eat again.

'I wish you'd told me. I wish you'd cared enough about me to confide in me. You say that I'm one of your closest—friends, and yet you never told me something as important as your having been married and divorced. It would have helped me to understand why you've been holding me at arm's length.' He looked at her, his pleasant face serious. 'It doesn't make any difference, you know, to the way I feel. I still want to marry you—desperately.'

'I'm sorry.' Zara could only shake her head and look down at the table unhappily. 'I just don't want to get involved again yet.'

'But you already are involved, aren't you?'

'Well, in a way, I suppose. I'm certainly very fond of you, Richard, and I . . .'

'No, not with me,' he said impatiently. 'With the man who was here, Masterson. You're emotionally involved with him. I could see it in the way you looked and behaved towards one another. He's your lover, isn't he?' he asked in self-inflicting pain.

Zara gave an incredulous laugh. 'No, he most certainly is not! Why, he's the last man I'd ever want to have an affair with.' She swallowed, forcing herself to speak more calmly. 'The only emotion you saw, Richard, was intense dislike. There are reasons, which I won't go into, why I dislike him so much, and I assure you that the less I see of him the better. And I didn't invite him here this evening, if that's what you're thinking. That was entirely his own idea.'

'Yes, of course.' Richard stood up. 'I'm sorry, Zara, but I don't feel hungry any more, so if you'll excuse me I'll be getting along.'

'You don't believe me? But I've told you the truth, Richard,' she assured him, jumping to her feet.

'I'm sure you have, as you see it. But what's the old quotation about "protesting too much"? You may believe you dislike him, Zara, but you're already more than halfway towards falling in love with him. I'd be willing to take a bet that by the time I get back from Bahrein you and he will be lovers at least.'

'That isn't so!' Zara exclaimed angrily. 'You couldn't be more wrong.'

'No? Well, I certainly hope I'm proved wrong.' Turning away, Richard went into the hall to get his overcoat.

'You will be,' she assured him vehemently. 'Richard, don't go. Stay and finish your meal, please.'

He gave a short laugh. 'The times I've longed for you to ask me to stay! But not just for a meal.' His eyes stared down into hers. 'If you want to prove you really care about me—and that Masterson means nothing to you—then ask me to *really* stay, Zara. Ask me to spend tonight with you,' he pleaded urgently.

She was unable to answer him and quickly looked away so that he couldn't see the dismay in her eyes.

Richard gave a bitter laugh of self-mockery. 'I knew I was a fool to ask. But which one of us is it you're denying, I wonder—Masterson or me?'

Jerking open the door, he strode out, leaving Zara looking after him in consternation—but she made no attempt to call him back. She shut the door and went into the kitchen, sudden rage filling her at what had happened. If Heath hadn't taken it into his head to come round she and Richard would have spent a pleasant, peaceful evening together. Now she very much doubted if she would ever see Richard again. In a sudden burst of fury, Zara scraped the omelettes off the plates and into the waste disposal, too annoyed to want to eat alone.

Of all the stupid ideas! How could Richard possibly think she and Heath were lovers, of all things? It was absolutely ridiculous! Going into the sitting-room, Zara turned on the television set and dropped angrily into an armchair in front of it. But within a minute she turned it off and sat back, feeling unutterably low. And it was no good telling herself that the heartache was because she had quarrelled with Richard, because she knew very well that it wasn't. It was for a love lost long ago that had come back to touch a heart she had thought hard enough to withstand any assault on it.

An hour later the phone rang and Zara ran to pick it up, sure that it was Richard ringing to apologise. 'Richard?' she said eagerly.

But it was an entirely different male voice that said, 'So he's left, has he?'

She didn't pretend that she didn't know who it was. 'How did you get this number, Heath? It's ex-directory.'

'Memorised it when I was in your flat,' he told her laconically.

Pursing her lips in annoyance, Zara said shortly, 'So what do you want?'

'To apologise for intruding on you and your—er—friend. I hope I didn't cause too much of an interruption.' But he didn't sound at all sorry, quite the opposite in fact.

'Just why did you come here?' she demanded. 'You knew I wouldn't have dinner with you.'

Heath was silent for a moment, then he said slowly, 'Because I kissed you. That night I took you home. It confirmed a lot of things for me.'

Zara's heart turned a somersault at his words and the soft tone in which he had said them, but it was easy to harden it again and say shortly, 'It confirmed a lot of things for me, too. That you were unscrupulous, for example. Also that you're so egotistical that you think no woman can resist you. Well, I'm sorry to disappoint you, but I'm not interested in narcissistic men like you,' she told him insultingly.

There was a vibration of anger in Heath's voice as he said, 'I wonder why you take such great delight in being rude to me, Zara? Maybe there's a deep psychological reason somewhere.'

'Or could it be that I find you personally obnoxious?' she taunted him.

'Is that why Richard left?' Heath barbed in his turn.

'Were you as charming to him?'

'Richard has got nothing to do with this. You leave him out of it!'

'I suppose he's in love with you,' Heath went on sneeringly. 'I feel sorry for the poor devil. He'll get no joy from the relationship. Although I expect he'll go on hoping until he realises the truth. Or has he realised already?'

'How dare you?' Zara exclaimed heatedly, realising how near the truth he was. 'I'll have you know I can marry Richard any time I like!'

'Oh, sure. But you won't. Were you keeping him dangling on your line just in case you ever felt like hauling him in? Don't deceive yourself, Zara—something tells me you're fast becoming a man-hater.'

She gave a gasp of incredulous amazement. 'You're crazy! Just because I can't stand you it doesn't mean that I dislike all men.'

'So why me?' he asked quickly. 'What have I done to make you so anti? It's certainly nothing that I've done recently, so it must have been in the past. In those few weeks when we were seeing each other. What was it, Zara?' he said urgently. 'Tell me!'

Realising she had been trapped, Zara took a deep breath and counted to ten, her knuckles showing white as she held the phone. She mustn't let him suspect anything or her own trap would fail. So with a light laugh she said, 'Really, this is the weirdest conversation! Of course nothing happened in the past. Why, I can hardly remember that time. No, if you really want to know, what I objected to was the way you made a pass over that business lunch, and then had me invited to dinner at the Wards'. I'm afraid that kind of thing makes me very angry. And coming here uninvited tonight—well, I'm sorry if I was rude, but I must admit that Richard and I did row—he was upset when he saw you here, especially when you said I was expecting you. You do understand?'

She tried hard to make her voice sound reasonable so that he would accept her explanation, and he sounded quite different as he said, 'Yes, of course. And it's I who should be apologising. But that's what I intended to do when I picked up the phone. As you say, it all got out of hand somewhere along the line.' He paused, then went on, 'Zara, look, can we start again? Forget all this and just start over? You're one of the most fascinating women I've ever met and I'd like very much to get to know you again.'

'What about Richard?' she temporised.

'I don't think you're at all serious about him,' Heath said after a moment. 'You didn't appear to be.'

'Not everyone wears their emotions on their sleeves,' Zara answered carefully.

'No. But why not try coming out with me and see how you feel about me?'

'I'll think about it,' she answered non-committally, but kept him hooked by saying, 'And in the meantime I expect we'll see each other quite often at the office while you're doing the advertising campaign for us.'

There was a hint of amusement in Heath's voice as he said, 'That sounds as if you're putting me on trial.'

'Maybe I am.'

'Haven't we already gone further than that? We certainly did in the past.'

'Did we?' Zara said coolly. 'I don't remember. And anyway, you said you wanted to start from the beginning again. Goodnight, Heath.' And she put the phone down before he could delve back into reminiscences again.

Zara had told Colin he could handle the publicity campaign, but she was unable to stay detached from it, not only because she wanted to see how well Heath's agency kept up to their promises, but also because it was so important. The fun leisurewear market was growing and expanding and if she could break into it with her range of fashionable and colourful, rather than just serviceable, sports clothes, Zara was sure that she would be on to a continuous winner. So, with her usual careful attention to detail, she began checking with Colin on every stage of the preparation and then got so interested that she went to all the discussions on it. Mostly the discussions were with Heath's assistant, Eric Jennings, but sometimes he said he would have to refer back to Heath before making a decision, which annoyed Zara. 'Tell your boss to come himself if he can't delegate the decision-making,' she told Eric roundly.

Colin grinned at this and Zara glared at him, knowing full well that she hated to delegate responsibility in anything important to her. But maybe that was why she was now in the position of power and could make Heath jump to her bidding. Only it didn't quite work out that way. When she went to the next meeting Heath wasn't there either.

'Where's Mr Masterson?' she asked his assistant.

'He's busy on another contract at the moment, but he's given me a number to call in case we run into any difficulties, but he doesn't envisage any,' Eric told her.

'Oh, doesn't he?' Zara snapped. 'Well, that isn't good enough. Phone him now and tell him to get over here.'

The two men looked at each other, then Eric picked up the phone and got Heath on the line. 'Miss Layston wants you to attend the discussion,' he told him diplomatically. 'No, there's no problem. She just thinks you ought to be in on the meeting.' He listened for a second, then held the receiver out to Zara. 'Heath would like to speak to you.'

Zara took it and said peremptorily, 'Before you start making any excuses, I do not see any point in holding a meeting when Eric has to refer every decision back to you as he did last time. If this contract is so unimportant to you, you shouldn't have taken it on,' she added heatedly.

'It is important, Zara. But yours isn't our only contract, you must realise that. Your last discussion was to search out any problems and you'll find that these have now been dealt with. Eric is quite capable of dealing with anything that arises today and I . . .'

'That isn't good enough,' she interrupted. 'Our contract specifies personal supervision throughout, so just get yourself over here. I'm not going to waste my time by having this meeting otherwise.'

Then she handed the receiver back to Eric, saying, 'I'm going to my office. Let me know when Heath arrives,' and strode out of the room before they could think of anything to say to stop her.

Back in her own office, Zara unlocked the safe and took a file from it. It was the report from the investigation agency on Heath and his company; it had only arrived that morning, brought by hand, and she hadn't had time to look at it yet. But Heath's absence from the meeting having given her a free period, now seemed as good a time as any. She looked at the report on his company first. It was a comprehensive one giving details of its financial status, the staff, everything she wanted to know in fact. It was a company with limited liability, Heath being the major shareholder and the other shares being divided between several other people, some of whom Zara took to be members of Heath's family as they bore the same surname. She grimaced, but had expected as much— Heath was bound to have a controlling interest. But she still stood a chance of getting a foothold into his agency by buying up some of the shares. It might well be worth a try. Putting through a call to her stockbroker, she instructed him to see if he could buy into the agency without divulging her name or interest.

Then she turned to the personal report on Heath. It enclosed a copy of the curriculum vitae he had submitted when applying for his last job—the one in America. It gave his date of birth, details of his education and experience up to that point. And it was impressive; Zara wasn't surprised that he had got the job. There was also a letter from his American employers giving him a most glowing reference. But it was the personal details in which Zara was the most interested. The report stated that he was unmarried, was heterosexual, had no outstanding debts, and did not gamble or drink to excess. It told her where Heath lived and that his neighbours had been questioned. He did not hold wild parties but had people round to dinner or the odd cocktail party. It also stated that he had women who quite often stayed overnight but that he did not seem to have a fiancée, or have had a steady girl-friend during the last year.

The fact that he hadn't married rather surprised Zara; he was so attractive to women, so arrantly masculine, that she thought he would have been hooked long ago. He was thirty-five now, and not exactly a playboy—he worked too hard for that, but it looked as if he might be turning into a confirmed bachelor. Zara's mouth tightened; if the way he had taken off after she had told him she loved him was anything to go by, then marriage was the only thing in life that scared the hell out of him! But the procession of girls to his door obviously meant that he was enjoying a hearty sex life for all that. A bitter look came into Zara's eyes as she remembered the passes he had made at her recently. Perhaps he was regretting that he hadn't taken her when he had the opportunity, seven years ago. Did he really expect her to fall in with his wishes—and into his bed—and become just another name on his list of conquests? To be enjoyed today and forgotten tomorrow? Her hand drumming on the desk, Zara vowed that Heath not only wouldn't forget her, he would go on regretting that he had ever met her for the rest of his life!

The internal phone rang and Mac told her that Heath had arrived, so she went back to Colin's office. It was raining heavily and Heath's hair clung wetly to his head, beads of raindrops on his high cheekbones like tears. Zara felt a sudden overpowering urge to lick them from his skin, and had to hastily turn and ask Colin to send for some coffee, her heart thumping so hard it was difficult to breathe.

Heath gave her an impatient look. 'I'm afraid I'm

pushed for time,' he said shortly. 'Shall we get on with the discussion?'

The four of them sat round a large table, the drawings and plans spread out before them, and began to go through the list of queries from the last meeting. As Heath had promised, they had all been dealt with, and he went on to deal as efficiently with queries that arose from the next phase of the campaign. Zara went through the photographs that had been taken of their tracksuits to pick the ones she wanted to use in the campaign, but said, 'What about the beachwear photographs? I don't see those?'

Heath made a rueful gesture towards the windows. 'It hasn't stopped raining or snowing for the last three weeks. Our photographic department have got all the models on call and are just hanging on for some decent weather to take them.'

'We don't have that long,' Zara reminded him rather uneasily.

'No, I know. But don't worry, if it comes to it we'll just have to simulate a beach in the studios.' He gave her a quick smile. 'Just keep your fingers crossed for fine weather.'

Her own eyes smiled in return. 'I've often noticed that people who sit around with their fingers crossed hoping for their luck to change don't get a lot of work done.'

Heath laughed. 'Maybe you're right at that.' He gave her a slightly challenging look. 'I trust that you're satisfied with the way I've answered your queries?'

That this was an indirect dig at her for insisting that he attend the meeting Zara was well aware. She gave him a cool look. 'As our contract guarantees your personal attention I should expect nothing less. I trust you intend to be at all future discussions on the campaign?'

'I'm doing my best to get most of my other work out of the way so that I can concentrate entirely on your contract,' he answered smoothly.

'Good. Because that's what we're paying for,' she told him, returning his mocking look with an equally sardonic one of her own.

Colin looked from one to the other of them and stood up, saying to Eric, 'If you'll come with me I'll get you those additional samples from the sportswear range that you wanted.'

Their two assistants having made a timely withdrawal, Heath looked across the table at Zara. 'Is your boy-friend back yet?'

'If you mean Richard then no, he isn't.'

'And have you thought any more about—us?'

Standing up, Zara went over to a side table to pour herself out another cup of coffee. 'Not particularly, no.'

Heath came to stand beside her, his hands thrust into his trouser pockets. 'So I suppose there's no point in asking you to have dinner with me?'

She reminded herself that she didn't want to antagonise him too much. She remembered, too, the raindrops on his cheeks. Putting down the cup, she slowly turned to face him, her hands gripping the edge of the table behind her. 'Why don't you ask and find out?' she replied with just a hint of husky provocativeness.

His eyes widening a little, Heath took his hands from his pockets and put one on either side of her slim waist, then they tightened as he leant forward to kiss her.

Zara stood perfectly still, letting him do what he wanted to her mouth, her lips slightly open, soft and yielding. But she made no attempt to respond, so that when he lifted his head he looked at her quizzically. 'Well, at least you didn't try to hit me again! So—will you have dinner with me?'

Her eyes fixed on the region of his tie, Zara somehow nodded and said, 'Yes.' He opened his mouth to speak, but she added quickly, 'A business dinner. On my expense account.'

Heath threw back his head and laughed. His eyes glistening with amusement, he said, 'I should have known. Don't you think about anything but work?'

'Not much,' Zara replied honestly.

His hands were still on her waist, and she was very aware of his touch, of his closeness. 'Richard can't be very important to you, then?' Heath guessed.

'No,' she acknowledged, looking him steadily in the eye. 'No man is important to me.' He frowned, trying to understand exactly what she meant, but she looked away. 'Weren't you in a hurry?' she reminded him.

'I was—but it can wait for this.' And this time he pulled her to him, moulding her body against his as he kissed her, his lips more demanding now as he sought to arouse an answering fire in her. Zara hesitated, but then her arms slowly rose to rest on his shoulders. Lifting his head a little, Heath looked into her face and saw that her eyes were open. He put his hand behind her neck and kissed her in a sudden fierce surge of passion, his lips hard on her own, but he kept his eyes fixed on her face until her body quivered suddenly and she closed her eyes, her mouth opening under his.

The sound of voices in the corridor outside made

Heath let her go and step back. Zara turned to pick up
her cup of coffee, her hands unsteady, and was
drinking it when Colin and Eric came back into the
room. Heath was busily picking up his papers and he
and Eric Jennings left almost immediately, leaving
Zara and Colin to talk over a few details before Zara
went back to her own office. When she got there she
went into her cloakroom and carefully re-made up her
mouth, the while trying not to look at the reflection of
the rest of her face. She didn't want to see the flush on
her pale cheeks or the banked fires of urgent need in
her green eyes. To do so would be to admit that she had
enjoyed Heath's kisses, and she must never, never do
that.

She had a date that evening, but when she got home
and played back her answerphone she found that
Heath had rung. 'Just to fix a date for our business
dinner,' he had said in an amused voice. 'I shall be out
of the office most of tomorrow, but you can reach me
on this number in the evening.' And he gave the
number she already knew to be of his flat.

But Zara, too, was busy. One of her new shops was
soon to be opened and she went to stay in the area so
that she could supervise the amount of stock to be sent
to it and its display, plus attending the interviews for
the new trainee under-manager and shop staff. One of
her more experienced managers was to be in charge of
it for the first year, but Zara liked to know exactly who
was in her employ. She also had to pay a visit to the
textile mill and combined it with a brief visit to Mr
Webster to keep him up to date on everything that was
happening. Not only because it was courteous to do so
but because they both got a great deal of delight out of

seeing each other and in discussing how well Panache was growing. So Zara had her secretary call Heath and arrange a time and place for their dinner date, not going back to London until the day she was due to met him.

She had her hair done and dressed with the care—she told herself—that she would have taken if she were going out with someone she liked. At seven-thirty her doorphone rang and she told Heath that she would be right down. It was still cold, but he wasn't wearing an overcoat over the evening suit that set her heart fluttering again in remembrance. But she managed to greet him with a cool smile and said, 'It was kind of you to come for me, but I could quite easily have met you at the restaurant, you know.'

Heath glanced at her as he helped her into his car. 'Don't be silly,' he said laconically.

Rather to her surprise, he drove out of London, taking the motorway for several miles before pulling off it and driving through countryside until they came to a large Georgian house standing in its own grounds that had been converted into a hotel and restaurant. For once it wasn't raining, but it was still cold, and they hurried inside. Here it was warm and pleasant, with a log fire burning in the Adam fireplace. Heath helped her off with her coat and slowly handed it to the waiting receptionist as he looked her over.

'You were wearing a velvet dress like that on the night that I first met you,' he told her, his voice sounding a little strange. 'Only it was green, not black.'

'Was I? I'm surprised that you remember after so long.'

'On the contrary, I remember everything about that

night,' Heath said softly, his eyes openly caressing.

Bright spots of colour showed in her pale cheeks, but
Zara turned quickly away so that he couldn't see and
walked ahead of him into the bar. She didn't know why
she had chosen this dress; she had been looking in her
wardrobes for something warm to wear and her hand
had somehow gone straight to it, wondering if he
would remember. Well, now she had her answer,
though whether it gave her satisfaction or not she
didn't know. The waiter handed them menus and
brought them an aperitif so that she could chat safely
about food and give herself time to recover a little.

The dining-room was newly decorated and rather
over-ornate, but the food was superb, the tables well
spaced out so that they could talk in comfort, and the
service discreetly attentive. For a while they talked
inconsequentially, as two people who didn't know each
other very well would, Heath telling Zara about his
time in America and she in turn telling him something
of the way she and Mr Webster had built up Panache.

'You said that Webster retired, I think?'

'Did I? Yes, about eighteen months or so ago. He
went to Spain for a long holiday with his new wife, but
now he's back in England.'

'His new wife?' Heath looked at her in surprise.

'Yes.' Zara's eyebrow rose sardonically. 'Just what
ideas did you have about Mr Webster and me?'

Heath shook his head. 'Nothing specific. I was just
surprised that someone of that age should have
married, that's all.'

Like hell, Zara thought, but she let it go and talked
of something else. When they had finished their main
course she sat back in her chair, feeling more at ease

and appreciating her surroundings. Feeling Heath's eyes on her she looked across at him and raised a questioning eyebrow.

'I was just thinking,' he said with a half-smile, 'how much you've changed and yet how little. In looks you've hardly altered at all—oh, lost a little puppy fat maybe, so that one can see how fine-boned you are. And you've acquired an outward gloss, but apart from that . . .' He shook his head. 'No, it's inside that you've changed.'

'Really?' said Zara in a dry tone that was meant to shut him up. 'What pudding are you going to choose?'

But, 'You've lost your spontaneity,' Heath went on. 'You used to be so warm—so loving,' he added deliberately. His eyes darkened. 'Your husband ought to be shot for doing that to you.'

'My hus . . .!' Zara stared at him open-mouthed. Then her face hardened. 'Leave my husband out of this. He has nothing to do with you.'

'All right,' Heath said evenly. He had been leaning forward, but now he sat back, his eyes on her face. 'But let's stop pretending that this is nothing but a business meeting, shall we? That isn't why I wanted to see you again, and you know it.'

'But it *is* why I wanted to see you,' Zara corrected him shortly. She looked at him, her green eyes glittering. 'Because I have a proposition to put to you.'

His lips twitched a little. 'A proposition?'

'Yes. I'm thinking of expanding my shops even further and going into home furnishing; wallpaper, curtains, bedlinens, that kind of thing. And all of them of course co-ordinated. I may even do carpets.' His interest aroused, Heath was giving her his whole attention. Taking a deep breath, Zara said, 'I want someone to do a feasibility study, taking into account the locations of our present shops and the ones that I have in mind for the future. And if I decide to go ahead, then I would of course require another large advertising campaign.'

Giving a low whistle of surprise and admiration, Heath sat up straight in his chair. 'You really believe in going places, don't you? And do you want me to do this feasibility study?'

'Could you guarantee to give me an unbiased report, bearing in mind that the advertising contract would probably go to you if I'm satisfied with the way you handle the Game, Set and Match campaign?'

Heath gave her a level look. 'Yes, I could.'

Strangely enough she believed him, but she didn't let him see that, instead giving him a small smile. 'I would, however, like some in-built guarantees. I would require Colin Royle, the head of my marketing department, you remember, to be closely concerned with the feasibility study and to have access to your findings at all times. And also,' she paused, her heart thumping a little now that the testing moment had come, 'as my company would be investing so much of our future success in your agency's hands then I should need written guarantees that Panache's interests would be placed ahead of any other contracts you take on, and again that you would give us your personal attention. And I should also require a small shareholding in your agency so that I could ensure my company's interests were being well served.' She held up a hand as Heath went to speak. 'I know what you're going to say, and I agree that it's unusual. But in return we're willing to draw up a very favourable contract. And please bear in mind that Panache is going places and you could come with us.'

Heath didn't answer at once, but after a moment he said, 'You were right; this certainly is a business dinner!' For a moment he looked rueful, then became practical again. 'I need hardly ask whether you've looked into the financial side of my agency. You must know that I hold a fifty-one-per-cent interest. If I sold you any of my shares I could possibly lose control.'

'Yes, I have,' Zara admitted. 'But I took it to be largely other members of your family and friends who hold the other shares. Perhaps they would agree to sell?'

'Do I take it that the sale of these shares to you is a condition of my doing the feasibility study—and getting the later contract?'

'Yes, it is.'

Picking up his glass, Heath took a drink. 'That sounds remarkably like blackmail, Zara.'

She shrugged. 'With something as important as this I want total commitment. This way I ensure that I get it.'

'How many shares would you want?'

'Ten per cent,' Zara replied promptly.

'And do I get any Panache shares in return?'

'I'd be willing to let you have the equivalent value,' she told him, knowing full well that she had a hundred per cent ownership and couldn't possibly lose control of the company.

'But not percentage?'

'Hardly. I should imagine that they're far from being the equivalent in value share for share.'

'No.' Heath took another drink, his eyes on her face.

'All right,' he said abruptly, 'I agree. I'll have my solicitor start to draw up the necessary papers straight away.'

Zara sat back in her chair, her hands gripped together in her lap, trying to keep the triumph out of her eyes. Heath had just taken the first step into the web she had spun, and soon he would be too far enmeshed ever to escape from the trap.

CHAPTER FIVE

THEY discussed the project in some detail, Heath catching some of Zara's excitement. He was full of ideas, too, which fuelled her enthusiasm, so that their coffee grew cold as they batted ideas to one another. It was the kind of stimulating discussion that Zara revelled in, making her eyes and face glow as she talked eagerly. They were both leaning forward across the table as vague suggestions became concrete possibilities. But then Heath laughed and caught hold of her gesticulating hand. 'Hey, slow down! We'll have forgotten half of this by the morning.' He smiled at her animated face. 'You know, I was beginning to think you only come alive when you get angry, but I see I was wrong.' He looked round. 'We seem to be the last here. Shall we go?'

Zara looked round in surprise, she hadn't even noticed that the room had emptied. 'Yes, of course.'

A waiter was hovering nearby, the bill already made out, and she beckoned him over, but Heath took the bill himself. 'No,' he said firmly. 'Business or not, this was my idea.'

She half opened her mouth to protest, but then shrugged. 'Okay, thanks,' and went to the cloakroom to collect her coat, automatically adding a spray of perfume and a touch more lipstick before she remembered who she was with. Which just showed how deeply interested she had been in their discussion if she could have forgotten *that*!

But she was fully aware of Heath again during the drive back to London, although they didn't talk very much until he drew up outside her flat. Then he turned to her. 'Well, it hasn't quite worked out the way I expected it to, but it's been a very stimulating evening for all that.'

'Oh? You mean you didn't believe me when I said it was to be a business meeting?'

'No.' He slid his arm along the back of her seat. 'What I had in mind was that we would just talk, get to know one another again. Perhaps talk about old times.' He paused, then added deliberately, 'And maybe find the answers to some questions that have been puzzling me about you.'

Zara turned her head away. 'I don't like talking about the past,' she said shortly. 'The present and the future are all that matters.'

Heath gave her a shrewd look. 'Does that really work—trying to shut out the past? I should have thought that our pasts are what has made us the people we are now.'

Slowly Zara turned her head to look at him again, a bitter smile on her lips. 'Yes,' she agreed, 'the past has made me *exactly* what I am now.' Heath, sensing her unhappiness, reached out a hand to cover hers, but she drew it quickly away. 'When can you start on the feasibility study?' she asked abruptly.

He laughed, but accepted the change of subject. 'It will mean taking on more staff, but that shouldn't be too difficult, and I might need more people when we do your home furnishing promotions. I've already taken on extra staff to do the present advertising campaign and I'll probably try to keep them on. So shall we say in a couple of weeks?'

'Fine.' Zara put her hand on the door catch. 'Thanks again for dinner. Goodnight.'

'Hey!' Heath caught her arm. 'Aren't you going to ask me up for a nightcap?'

'No.'

'It would be much warmer in your flat,' he coaxed.

'No.'

He sighed. 'You're a hard woman, Zara.' Drawing her to him, he kissed her insinuatingly, then drew away. 'I think you must be made of ice. You don't even melt when I kiss you.'

'Is that what I'm supposed to do?'

He smiled a little, his finger running gently over her lips. 'It would be—encouraging.'

'Maybe I don't want to encourage you.'

'So I gathered.' But that didn't stop him from putting his arms round her and kissing her again, kissing her so thoroughly that the familiar ache of longing shot through her so fiercely that she almost moaned aloud, and it took all her will-power not to surrender to him as he wished. 'When can I see you again?' he asked huskily when he at last raised his head, adding before she could speak, 'And I don't mean a business meeting. I want us to spend some time together without even thinking about work. I want to concentrate on just us— as people. As a man—and a very attractive woman.'

He nuzzled her neck as he spoke and gently bit her ear-lobe, his closeness making her bite her teeth together to stop herself giving way to the growing yearning inside. 'We can't—separate ourselves like that,' she stammered.

Putting her hands on his shoulders, she tried to push him away, but Heath slipped his hands inside her loose coat and began to caress her. 'I can,' he said thickly.

'Don't! Don't do that.' She pulled violently away from him, hitting the back of her head on the window. 'Don't touch me!'

Heath drew back, staring at her. 'Zara, what is it? I don't . . .'

But she had pulled open the door and stumbled out of the low car, was searching feverishly in her bag for her key. Getting out of the car, Heath stood on the other side of it. 'It's all right,' he said brusquely. 'I get the message.'

Zara bit her lip, realising that he must think her absolutely crazy. 'I'm sorry,' she managed to say. 'It's just that—that I don't like being handled.'

For a moment they stared at each other across the frost-covered roof of the car, then Zara turned, let herself into her building, and ran quickly up to her flat.

Richard came home a couple of days later, but Zara was away on business again and didn't see him until the weekend. She welcomed him warmly, making his face brighten with pleasure, and they spent an extremely pleasant evening at the theatre, going afterwards for supper to one of London's famous fish restaurants. 'We ought to eat more fish and vegetarian food,' Zara told him as they drove back to her flat. 'It's much better for you.'

'You're not going on one of those health-food kicks, are you?' he asked as they went inside. 'You're thin enough already. I like you as you are.'

Pulling her to him, he kissed her, and she gave a little

sigh. 'I'm glad you're back, Richard.'

'Are you? Really?' She murmured agreement and he smiled down at her. 'And there's nothing between you and Heath Masterson?'

'No, nothing. Let's have a drink and put some music on.' Breaking free of his hold, Zara went over to the music centre. 'I feel like something light. How about this?' She put on a disc of movie themes and turned the volume up.

'Good lord, that's much too loud!' Richard came over and turned it down, then watched her as she began to dance around the room, a glass in her hand. At first he looked amused, but his smile slowly faded, leaving him watching her intently. Catching hold of her wrist, he made her stop and pulled her close against him. She laughed. 'No, come and dance.'

But Richard kissed her more fiercely than he had ever done before, then said urgently, 'Zara, I want you so much. I'm not going to let you put me off any longer. I'm going to stay with you tonight.'

Immediately she pulled free from his hold. 'Wait till you're damn well invited!'

'*I have waited,*' Richard said vehemently. 'I've been waiting for months for you to make up your mind. I've asked you to marry me time and time again, but you've always put me off. But now I want a straight answer, Zara. I want to know whether you'll marry me—or failing that whether you'll commit yourself enough for us to become lovers?' he demanded harshly, his face red with anger.

'Why now? Why must you have an answer tonight, Richard?'

'Because my patience has worn out. And because I

think your feelings for Masterson are deeper than you admit.'

Well, that was true enough, Zara owned inwardly; only Richard suspected her of entirely opposite emotions. Trying to be calm, she went over and turned off the music, then faced him again. 'Richard, I've told you before that I'm not ready to marry again yet. I'm very fond of you and I . . .'

'Fondness isn't enough,' he said shortly. 'I want a total commitment, Zara.'

Slowly she shook her head. 'Then I'm sorry, but I can't give you that. Not yet. But I'd be very happy to go on as we are.'

His face going pale, he said, 'A platonic friendship isn't what I have in mind.' Making one last desperate try, he said, 'Zara, even if you don't love me we could still enjoy being—close to each other. Maybe love would grow out of that.'

'Maybe it would,' she agreed after a moment. 'But I'm sorry, I can't guarantee that, and right now I can't offer you more than friendship.'

'I see.' He straightened up, his back very stiff. 'So it's goodbye, then. I suppose I've seen this coming for some time, but I've always hoped . . .' He broke off and shrugged himself into his coat. 'Don't bother to come to the door,' he said bitterly. 'You've shown me out often enough—this time I'll go of my own accord.'

Zara watched him go with regret, she had enjoyed the times that they had spent together, but there was also a small inner feeling of relief; Richard had been getting too serious and she had no time for emotional involvement, especially when she wanted to concentrate on getting her revenge on Heath. And with this in mind the first thing she did when she went into the office on Monday morning was to call her stockbroker. 'Is there any news on the Masterad shares?' she asked eagerly.

'We've looked into it, Miss Layston, and we've found that the forty-nine per cent of shares not owned by Heath Masterson are divided between several people including an uncle and an aunt of his. The aunt and uncle aren't married to each other, by the way. We think that the easiest way to buy some shares might be by approaching the aunt, who is elderly and might be willing to sell. She owns fifteen per cent. Would you like us to make enquiries on your behalf?'

'Please, but not mentioning my name, of course, although I want them for my private portfolio. And perhaps you could approach the others too. I want to buy as many as I can. What is the value of the shares at the moment?'

They discussed the financial side of it for a few minutes, Zara surprising the stockbroker by the amount she was willing to pay. But the deal of Heath's ten per cent of shares in exchange for some in Panache was already taking place and if she could get even another fifteen per cent, it would give her a very decisive voice in Masterads' dealings.

She had a meeting that day with the heads of her three textile factories, and as there were some present problems to be solved and new ideas to be planned for, the meeting went on all day and she didn't get back to her office until quite late. Mac had been holding the fort for her as usual and presented her with a formidable list of phone messages. As she glanced down it, Heath's name immediately caught her attention.

'What did Masterads want?'

'It was a personal call from Mr Masterson; when I told him you were busy he said he would call you at home tonight. Oh, by the way, I've got the papers here for you to sign to complete the exchange of shares.'

'Good, I'll do that right away.' She signed the papers with a small smile of satisfaction. 'You get along home now, Mac. Thanks for taking care of things for me. See you tomorrow.'

Mac went off willingly, eager to get home to his house in the suburbs where his wife and two young children were waiting for him. But for Zara her day still hadn't finished, there was the list of messages to deal with as well as several letters that had arrived by the second post. Some of the things she was able to deal with quickly and easily, but others demanded more time and attention. At eight she suddenly decided that she had had enough; she would go home and get something to eat and then deal with the rest at home. Putting the rest of the papers into her briefcase, she stretched tiredly, realising that she had been sitting down all day. She could do with some fresh air and exercise, but had such a busy schedule for the coming week that there was little chance of finding the time for it.

It was raining again, as it had spasmodically for the past month. Zara couldn't remember a more miserable end to winter, the only consolation being that all the weather prophets were forecasting a very hot summer to make up for it. She paused on the step outside the main entrance to put on a jaunty rain-hat to match her mac—a Panache outfit, of course. The building was situated in what had once been an old mews about a quarter of a mile from Oxford Street, and she knew from experience that she would have to walk up to the busy main street before she would find a free cab, if she was lucky enough to find one in this weather. But as she stepped out on to the pavement she heard someone call her name and looked across the road to see Heath just getting out of his car. He came quickly over to her. 'Want a lift?' he asked with a grin.

She hesitated for a moment too long, giving him time to grab her hand and hurry her across to his car. Once inside he raised a questioning eyebrow. 'Home?'

She nodded and said, 'Were you waiting for me?'

Heath, his eyes on the road as he threaded his way through the traffic, gave a brief nod. 'Yes. I saw your light on in your office and guessed you were working late, so I thought I'd hang around for a while.'

'Why?' Zara asked suspiciously, afraid he might have got wind of her wanting to buy his agency's shares.

But Heath merely smiled. 'Because I wanted to save you a walk in the rain, of course.'

It wasn't far to her flat. Heath pulled up outside and came to open the door for her. She started to thank him for the lift, but her voice died in her throat as she looked up into his face. His eyes were warm but slightly mocking and his jaw was thrust determinedly forward. Putting his hand under her elbow, he firmly walked her over to the door and went up to her flat with her.

There, as if sensing her tiredness, he began to take over, hanging their coats in the hall cupboard and quite naturally walking over to the drinks trolley and pouring out a couple of gin and tonics. 'Cheers,' he toasted, handing her a glass.

Zara took the glass from him, her eyes on his face. 'Look, I don't know what you expect from coming here, but I've brought a lot of work home with me to do.'

'I don't *expect* anything,' he told her. 'Have you eaten yet?'

'No, but I . . .'

'Then you're in luck, because I'm going to fix you one of my special meals. Which way is the kitchen?'

'Hey, now wait a minute——' Zara began to protest.

But Heath came over and put his hands on her shoulders. 'Relax,' he said softly. But then his face hardened a little. 'Unless you mean that Richard is likely to turn up again. Do I make a meal for three instead of two?'

'No.'

His dark eyes became intent. 'That sounded a very definite no.'

'Yes, it was.'

'Because he's away on business again?'

'No, he isn't away.'

'I see.' His hands tightened for a moment, but then he nodded and became brisk again. 'Okay, so it's dinner for two.' Taking off his jacket, he took out his cuff links and turned back his shirt sleeves. 'Now, where's the kitchen?'

'Over there.' Zara gestured in some amusement. 'Are you trying to tell me you can really cook?'

'You shall be the judge of that in about half an hour or so. Now go and take it easy until I call you,' he ordered.

Zara didn't, of course, instead going into her study to

continue working, dictating the gist of letters for Mac to do the following day, checking over the contract of a shop they were buying, making notes and suggestions for a proposal to have a store within a store in New York, besides a lot of more mundane work.

It was nearly three-quarters of an hour before Heath came to find her. 'Dinner's ready,' he told her.

'Mm, I just have to finish this.'

But he firmly took the pen out of her hand. 'It'll spoil if you don't come at once.'

She gave him an indignant look, but then laughed and stood up. 'That sounds as if it ought to be my line.'

'Not tonight. Your turn next. Come on, I'm hungry!'

He had found her crystal candle-holders and put short fat red candles in them. That, and a couple of lamps, was the only light in the dining-room. He handed her into her chair, brought the first course from the kitchen and poured out some wine. It was, Zara noted, one of her good bottles, proving that he knew his wines. He had made mushroom soup, laced, if Zara wasn't mistaken, with sherry. She tried it warily, Heath grinning at her expression. 'Okay?'

She nodded. 'It's good.'

'Don't sound so surprised. I've been looking after myself for quite some years now.'

'You've never married?' she asked with studied casualness.

'No. But then you already know that.'

'Do I?'

'Oh, yes. You found it out when you had that investigation done on me.'

There was no point in lying; he wouldn't believe her anyway. 'How did you find out?' she asked ruefully.

'The people I worked for in America got in touch with me. They said they'd been asked for a detailed reference about me and they thought I was applying for a new job. So they asked me to go back to them.'

'I see.' Zara shrugged. 'It was natural for us to want to know all about you when we were putting so much business in your hands.'

'Fair enough,' Heath agreed, but then his voice hardened. 'But was it also necessary to question my neighbours and the staff of my company about my personal life?'

'Did the investigation agency go that far?' Zara pretended to be surprised.

'I'm quite sure you know they did,' he answered shortly, 'Why go to those lengths, Zara?'

She shrugged noncommittally. 'I didn't give any specific instructions; I just asked for a report on you and your company. It was just a safeguard, that's all.' She gave him a quick glance under her lashes. 'I'm sure you've had a report done on my company as well.'

Heath gave a short laugh. 'No, I haven't. I happen to believe in making my own judgements. And also in trust. Although you evidently don't.'

Zara's face tightened and for an instant her eyes filled with hate. 'I have no reason to put any faith in people's promises,' she flashed at him. 'And I certainly don't put any trust in . . .' She stopped hastily, aware that she might say something she would regret. 'The soup was delicious,' she said instead. 'What's next?'

With a rather wry smile, Heath said, 'Boeuf Bourguignon and rice. You don't have an awful lot of food in stock to work with.'

'I eat out a lot,' Zara explained. 'And unless I'm

entertaining I usually just make an omelette or something.'

She half rose to pick up the empty soup bowls, but Heath waved her back. 'I'll do it.'

He came back with the Boeuf Bourguignon and ladled it on to their plates. Zara watched him and was filled with a sudden surge of sadness; how much she had wanted this seven years ago, what she wouldn't have given then to be his wife and have spent evenings together like this! But she had offered him the only thing she had—herself. And that he had spurned without even bothering to tell her. She sat silently looking blindly down at her plate.

'Perhaps you'd like me to taste it first to make sure it doesn't poison you,' Heath offered.

'What?' She looked up and blinked. 'Sorry, I was thinking of something else.'

'Penny for them, then.' He lifted his hand. 'But I'm not paying if you were thinking about work.'

Zara forced herself to smile. 'I'm short a penny, then.' She gave him a direct look. 'Why did you wait for me tonight? What do you want from me, Heath?'

'What makes you think I want something?'

'Men always want something from a woman,' she answered shortly.

Heath nodded slowly. 'Yes, I suppose that's true enough.' He paused, then said, 'What I want from you at the moment, I suppose, is more evenings like this, talking, getting to know one another. I'd like for us to go out together, be friendly, companionable, and yet stimulate each other too. I want—I guess I want us to be at ease with one another.'

As she listened to him, Zara's face slowly tightened.

'I never feel at ease with you,' she said abruptly.

'Why not?' he asked, his voice soft but urgent.

She shrugged. 'I don't know.'

'Because of the past? Because of what we meant to each other before?'

'I told you,' she said shortly, 'I don't like talking about the past. And come to think about it, I don't like people coming here unless I give them a specific invitation. And that *does* apply to you.'

But Heath wasn't in the least put out. 'And deprive yourself of meals like this? You're a fool to yourself, Zara my darling.'

'Very likely,' she agreed. 'And don't call me that!'

'Is there anything else you want to stop me doing?' he asked with a mock patient air.

From breathing, she thought, but only said, 'I'll let you know.'

They finished their meal with coffee which they took into the sitting-room, leaving the dishes for her housekeeper to clear in the morning. Heath wasn't so emancipated that he insisted on doing the washing-up, she noticed. She put on a cassette and went to walk past him to an armchair, but he caught her wrist and drew her down beside him on the sofa. 'Did you and Richard quarrel?' he asked. 'Finally, I mean.'

'Mind your own business!'

'You're fond of saying that, aren't you? But when are you going to realise that you *are* my business?'

Zara looked away, part of her resenting the proprietorial way he had put his arm across her shoulders, resenting also the way he had taken over that evening, but part of her, too, was excited by it, her senses and emotions heightened by his nearness.

His fingers began to caress her neck gently as Heath said, 'There's an exhibition of Turner's watercolours opening at the Royal Academy this week. How about having lunch with me on Wednesday and taking an hour off to go round it?'

A gallery sounded a safe enough place, Zara thought, so she nodded. 'Yes, all right.'

He smiled at her in pleased surprise. 'I was certain you'd say you were busy or something.'

'Oh, I do take time off occasionally.'

'Good, I'm glad to hear it.' And his grip tightening, Heath pulled her forward to kiss her. 'You know,' he murmured when he let her go, 'I think the ice almost melted there for a moment.'

'Who wouldn't?' she answered with pretended flippancy. 'You're obviously very experienced.'

He nodded. 'True. I'm not denying it. And you must be, too, if you've been married.'

Zara turned her head away. 'The two things don't necessarily equate.'

Heath looked at her narrowly. 'Perhaps not.' He seemed about to ask a question, but then changed his mind. Instead he drew her to him again, saying, 'But you're still a very sexy lady.'

When he kissed her this time he moved his hands over her back, gently caressing her, but when his hand slid inside her sweater, Zara pulled away. 'It's getting late,' she said pointedly. 'And I still have work to do.'

Somewhat to her surprise, he immediately got to his feet. 'And I have an early start tomorrow. We're interviewing people for your feasibility study and I want to get as much of my other work done as possible before we start.'

'How many people are you taking on?'

'About ten, but most—perhaps all—of them will only be short-term, of course.' Going to the window, Heath pulled the curtain aside to look out and grimaced. 'It's still raining. Heaven knows when we'll get those swimwear photographs taken. If the sun doesn't shine during the next week we'll just have to do a studio mock-up.'

'I always think they don't ring true somehow.'

'I agree with you. But needs must in this weather.' Heath turned to face her. 'Goodnight, Zara.'

'Goodnight.'

She made no move to go to him, but Heath said softly, 'Come here and say goodnight properly.'

'No, I . . .'

'Come here,' he insisted.

Slowly, her eyes rebellious, Zara moved forward until she was close enough for him to touch her, but that was all.

'Okay. Now put your arms round my neck, stand on your tippytoes, say "goodnight, Heath" nicely, and kiss me.' He spoke as if he was instructing a small child, but his eyes smiled warmly, encouragingly.

'Oh, really, this is ridiculous! I . . .'

'Do it, Zara,' he insisted.

'Oh, for heaven's sake!' But she put her hands on his shoulders and reached up to kiss his mouth.

'You forgot to say goodnight, Heath,' he reminded her.

Striding out into the hall, Zara grabbed his overcoat out of the cupboard and thrust it at him. 'Goodnight, Heath,' she said on a raised note of anger.

Laughing, he took it from her. 'Goodnight,

sweetheart. I'll call for you at twelve on Wednesday.'

When he had gone, Zara immediately went back to her desk to finish her work, but was quite unable to concentrate. She kept wondering if it was remotely possible that Heath really was falling for her. On his past record it seemed most unlikely. Okay, maybe he did fancy her a little, but he was probably making up to her only because of who she was, because he wanted to continue to do business with her. Or perhaps because she was rich. It would be really ironic if he wanted to marry her now after he had run away from marriage with her before. Zara suddenly stabbed her pen down into her desk. I'd rather die than let him get his hands on a penny of the money I've worked so hard for! she thought fiercely. But it was necessary to let him go on thinking that she might be won round. She had to keep him sweet for just a few weeks longer until his company and his world crashed around him.

Strangely enough, Zara enjoyed herself on Wednesday, although it began far from auspiciously. Heath came to collect her at work as he had promised, but instead of waiting for her down in reception he came up to her office and gave her a possessive kiss of greeting right in front of Mac and one of the typists. She gave him a fuming look and would have refused to go with him if it wouldn't have created a scene. 'How dare you do that?' she demanded furiously as soon as they were outside.

'Because I wanted to, of course,' Heath answered outrageously.

She turned to glower at him. 'And just who the hell do you think you are? Do you realise it will be all round the company within hours?'

He grinned down at her. 'Stop being so priggish—or I'll do it again right here on the pavement.'

Zara opened her mouth to say, 'You wouldn't dare,' then shut it again hastily when she saw the gleam in his eyes. He grinned again. 'Much wiser,' he told her. 'Come on, my car's parked on a yellow line.'

But when they reached it Heath gave a groan of annoyance when he saw that a traffic warden, one of London's meter maids, had already spotted it. Going across, he put Zara solicitously into the car and then started talking to the warden. Two minutes later he got in—and without a ticket. The traffic warden even stopped the traffic so that he could pull out!

Zara stared at him in dumbfounded amazement. 'How on earth did you manage that?'

'She couldn't resist my masculine charm, of course.' He gave her a sidelong look, then laughed. 'Don't ask, Zara. You'd never forgive me if you knew.'

'Oh! Why, you . . .' She glared at him for a moment, guessing what tale he must have spun, and then burst out laughing. 'You're incorrigible!'

'Of course.' He pulled up at a traffic light and turned to smile at her, his eyes caressing her face. 'Ah, I'd almost forgotten that lovely spontaneous laugh you had. I'm glad you've got it back.'

'I never lost it,' she said shortly, which wasn't at all true; there had been a period when she hadn't laughed for a *very* long time.

He took her to the Italian restaurant where they had eaten several times when they had first gone out together. At first Zara didn't recognise the place because it had expanded into the next-door building, but the proprietor was the same, greeting Heath by name and leading him to a table tucked away in an alcove, the same table they had always used.

Heath ordered drinks and smiled at her. 'Remember this place?'

'Vaguely,' she admitted. 'I seem to remember that the food was good.'

'It still is. What would you like?'

They ordered, and Zara said, 'How are you getting on with the feasibility ...'

But Heath leaned forward and put two fingers on her lips, silencing her. 'Oh no, you don't! This isn't a business lunch, it's purely social. We aren't going to mention work. Okay?'

She shrugged, sitting back so that he couldn't reach her. 'As you like,' she answered casually, but her heart beating rather fast from the surprise intimacy of his touch. 'Have you ever been to Italy?'

So they talked about travel and food, and other subjects where they could converse on a safe level, while Zara's heart was full of memories of the brief happiness of the past, memories that filled her with yearning and yet tore and hurt too. She didn't eat very much and Heath didn't seem very hungry either, so they quite soon went on to the Royal Academy and wandered round the rooms looking at the pictures. Heath bought a guide and read out some of the descriptions and history of the watercolours, Zara having to stand quite close to him to listen and very aware of him beside her. Sometimes they accidentally touched and she quickly moved away, flinching as if she had been stung. But once Heath deliberately took hold of her hand and wouldn't let her go when she tried to pull away.

'Why are you afraid?' he said softly, his eyes holding hers.

'Don't be silly!' she snapped, and jerking her hand out of his walked swiftly out of the building into the cold wintry wind.

Heath caught up with her as she began to walk across the forecourt towards the street. 'If you're not afraid why are you running away?' he demanded.

'I'm not. I have to get back to the office. I have an appointment at three.'

'How convenient,' he answered on a note of sardonic disbelief.

When they reached the street, Zara looked for a taxi, but there wasn't one in sight. 'Thank you for lunch,' she said formally.

'Thank you for coming. Will you have dinner with me on Friday evening?'

'No, sorry.' She saw that he was about to argue and said, 'I shall be away. If you remember one of our new shops is opening on Saturday morning and I have to be at the opening ceremony, and there's also going to be a small party for the staff the night before. I want to go to that too.'

'But you'll be back on Saturday evening? So have dinner with me then?'

Again she shook her head. 'Sorry, I have a date.'

Heath's face hardened. 'I thought you said it was all over with Richard?'

'It is.' She gave him a cool look. 'Richard isn't the only man I go out with.' She saw a taxi cruising along and lifted her arm, attracting the driver's attention. While she waited for him to do a U-turn and come alongside, she turned to Heath and gave him an unknowingly wanton look. 'Do you really think I live such a nun-like existence?' She laughed harshly. 'I'm an experienced divorcee, remember? I don't have to restrict myself to just one man.'

Heath's face grew taut. 'No, I don't suppose you do. As you say, you probably have plenty of escorts—plenty of opportunities.' He paused as the taxi came up to them. 'But somehow I doubt very much whether you ever take advantage of them, Zara.' He opened the cab door and held it for her, his eyes fixed on her face for a long moment before he slammed it shut and gave the driver the address of her office.

Zara sat still, her heart beating painfully, knowing it would soon be over and she would never have to see Heath again.

She really did have a date on Saturday evening; with an ex-colleague who was in London for a few days. It was purely platonic, the two of them merely enjoying each other's company, and Zara had a pleasant if unexciting evening. On Sunday, she half expected Heath to ring, but he didn't, and she didn't see him again until the Tuesday when he and Eric Jennings came over to the Panache building to describe how they intended to go about the feasibility study. Afterwards Heath made a point of being alone with her for a moment and asked her to go to the theatre with him the following evening, and rather to his surprise, Zara agreed. And she went out with him on the Friday night, too, although she was afraid that by doing so she might encourage him enough to make a pass at her. But Heath behaved like a perfect gentleman, paying her compliments admittedly, but contenting himself with just a couple of kisses when they said goodnight.

This reticent behaviour left Zara with very mixed feelings. She was relieved, of course, but she had fully expected to have to fight Heath off, and not having to came as rather an anti-climax. She began to wonder rather uneasily just what game he was playing, but comforted herself with the knowledge that he was stretching his financial resources to the limit to do the sportswear promotion and the feasibility study. It wouldn't be long now before she had him completely within her power.

On Monday morning she had further corroboration of this when her stockbroker rang her and rather excitedly told her that Heath's aunt had agreed to sell her shares in Masterads. 'And I think there's a good chance of being able to buy others too,' he told her. 'His uncle is definitely tempted by your offer, but the difficulty is that he talked about consulting Heath Masterson first. If he does that . . .' he paused, letting the implications sink in.

'Yes, I see what you mean,' Zara said. 'If Heath Masterson finds out that someone wants his uncle's shares, he'll check on the others and find that his aunt has sold.'

'Precisely. And then if he's wise he'll buy back the rest of the shares himself to make sure he has overall control.'

'If he has the money, or can raise it,' she agreed.

'That shouldn't be difficult when he tells the bank or finance company about his tie-in with you,' the stockbroker reminded her.

'Mm.' Zara smiled, realising that she had got Heath where she wanted him either way. But buying shares in his company would probably be the better alternative. She thought for a moment, her gaze on the bleak weather outside, then said, 'Maybe I can arrange for Masterson to be out of the country for a few days.'

'That would be very convenient. And if you could also arrange for him to go as soon as possible and to be kept occupied . . .'

Zara frowned thoughtfully, but then her brow cleared. 'I think I could do that. Yes, I think I could certainly keep him occupied. I'll call you and let you know when to go ahead.'

CHAPTER SIX

As Zara buckled her seat belt in the executive class of the plane taking them to Nassau she glanced at Heath sitting beside her and realised that getting him out of the country had been easier than she had dared to hope.

After she had spoken to her broker she had checked that the swimwear photographs still hadn't been taken, and then rung Heath.

'Well, hallo,' he greeted her. 'Is this business or social?'

'Business, I'm afraid. Heath, I'm getting worried about the swimwear photographs.'

'Yes, it doesn't look as if the weather is going to ease up, so I'm afraid we'll have to have them done in a studio, unfortunately.'

'I've been thinking about that,' she told him with studied casualness. 'I don't think studio photos would look right. So I really feel that we ought to send a photographic team somewhere hot and sunny right away.'

'That would be expensive,' Heath warned.

'Yes, I know, but this is an important promotion and I think we ought to afford it.'

'Where were you thinking of sending them?'

'To the Bahamas, perhaps. Or some place equally hot and exotic at this time of the year. And I would like you,' she added deliberately, 'to go with the team to make sure that everything goes all right.'

'Trying to get rid of me, Zara?' Heath asked with wry humour. 'Sorry, I've got too much on here. But don't worry, I'll make sure that the person in charge knows exactly what we want.'

'Oh, that's a shame. Well, at least I know what we want even though I don't know anything about photographic modelling, so at least I'll be able to supervise a little.'

His voice sharpened. 'You mean you intend to go along, too?'

'Yes, I thought I might. I've been working hard lately and this weather is getting me down. I could do with a break in the sun.'

'I see.' His voice growing thoughtful, Heath asked, 'When did you want the team to leave?'

'As soon as possible, I should think. How long do you think it would take to arrange?'

'As everyone's on standby waiting for the weather to change, only about three days. Luckily the Bahamas aren't part of the States, so we won't need visas. Can you manage it in three days?'

'Yes, I'll make sure I can.' She paused, and added on a carefully non-committal note that had just the slightest trace of wistfulness, 'I'm sorry you won't be coming with us.'

'Well, if you're organised enough to take a holiday at such short notice, then I ought to be able to as well. So maybe I will come along, after all.'

Yes, it had been as easy as that. She only had to dangle the bait and he had been instantly hooked. And now here they were, three days later, taking a flight to Nassau, the capital of the Bahamas, with two models, the photographer, his assistant, and a hairdresser-cum-make-up artist. Plus of course a whole large suitcase full of Panache swimwear and sportswear in the cargo hold. And back in London her stockbroker was negotiating to buy at least another sixteen per cent of Masterad shares, which would give her exactly the same holding as Heath himself now held.

The thought brought a smile to her lips, and Heath put his hand over hers on the armrest between them, saying, 'You look happier already.'

'Do I?' She gave an amused laugh, thinking just how mistaken he was. 'It must be the thought of all that sunshine. I can't wait to get on a beach and sunbathe!'

The take-off was smooth and easy and the stewardess soon brought round drinks and the menus for dinner. Heath had brought a briefcase stuffed with work with him and settled down to do it, while Zara leaned back in her seat and watched him mockingly. 'You ought to learn to delegate,' she told him.

He grinned and turned to her, his eyes darkening as they ran over her. 'Once this lot is out of the way my time will be my own—and yours,' he added meaningfully.

So Heath worked most of the time as they flew over the ocean below them, stopping only to eat, giving all his attention to the task. As Zara lay back in her seat, glancing through a fashion magazine, her eyes often strayed to his intent profile. He was so self-possessed, so sure of himself. But then he always had been. She wondered how he would react when he realised that she had deliberately set out to ruin him. He would be angry, she was sure, furiously angry, and for a moment Zara felt a lick of fear. But then she remembered the way he had walked out on her, only to take it for granted that she would once more fall into his arms the moment he came back into her life. Just as if nothing had happened.

Zara looked away into the brilliant blue of cloudless sky outside. Maybe all the unhappiness that she had gone through in her marriage hadn't been directly Heath's fault, but he had most certainly been responsible for the bitterness that had changed her character and driven her into it. And she was determined to make him pay for the cold-blooded way he had treated her.

They landed in the Bahamas late in the afternoon, and took a mini-bus to a hotel on Paradise Island, a small island to the north of Nassau given completely over to tourism and reached from the main town by a toll bridge. Nassau seemed a strange mixture of traditionalism and commercialism; the traffic all drove on the left-hand side of the road as it did in Britain, but the cars were all large, American models. Some of the buildings in the town were old colonial style, but once out of town there were big new hotels and developments everywhere.

Their hotel was situated on Paradise Beach, a long, curving stretch of palm-fringed white sand with the sound of waves breaking on the shore a perpetual rhythm in the background. After the cold of London it was heaven and, like the two models, Zara couldn't wait to get to her room to change into lighter clothes. They all had single rooms on the same floor with balconies overlooking the sea, Zara not having made any attempt to get a better room for either herself or Heath. But as it was, the room she had been given was perfectly adequate, with its own bathroom of course and a much larger than average single bed—almost a double, in fact. After taking off her coat, Zara went straight to the full-length window, pushed open the door and stepped on to the balcony, revelling in the warmth that was still in the air although it was early evening.

'Great, isn't it?'

She turned and saw that Heath had come out on to the balcony to the left of her own. 'It certainly is,' she agreed fervently. 'You don't realise how much you miss the sun until you come to it suddenly like this.' Lifting her face towards the glowing horizon, Zara closed her eyes, feeling the warmth on her skin, the light breeze from the sea lifting loose strands of her hair. Her lips parted a little in voluptuous contentment as she stood there for a couple of minutes just soaking up the sun, completely unaware of how sensuous she looked until she turned to go in and saw the naked flame of desire in Heath's eyes.

It was so intense that she gave a little gasp of surprise and recognition, her eyes widening.

'Zara . . .' Heath reached his hand out to her across the concrete wall dividing the balconies, but she stepped back, her hands close to her body protectively, then quickly turned and went back into her room.

The seven of them met again for dinner, sharing a table in the large hotel restaurant that overlooked the sea. Zara took good care that she sat at the opposite end from Heath, but those few seconds on the balcony seemed to have brought to the surface emotions that he had kept under tight control before. She was aware of his eyes on her and felt her own irresistibly drawn towards him, so that their glances often locked before Zara hastily looked away again, her heart beating painfully. One of the models, Gemma, a tall brunette chosen for her athletic figure, was sitting next to Heath and doing her best to amuse and captivate him, but she was wasting her time and soon realised it. She looked from him to Zara and shrugged her shoulders with a rather resentful grimace, then turned to devote herself to the good-looking young photographer's assistant on her other side who doubled as the male model when one was needed.

After dinner they all strolled down to the beach so that the photographer could get some idea of the shots he wanted to take in the morning. He was very enthusiastic and full of ideas. 'Of course the light out here is very strong,' he told Zara. 'I'll have to experiment a bit, but I can't help but get some good shots with the beach and the palm trees.'

He wanted to walk to Pirates' Cove, the next beach along, but the make-up girl reminded him that if the models didn't go to bed they would probably suffer from jet-lag and show it the next morning, so they went back to the hotel, saying a general goodnight as they separated to go to their rooms. But Heath and Zara's rooms were round a bend in the corridor from the others and when they reached it and were out of sight, he caught her arm. 'Zara, we have to talk. I . . .'

'No!' She bit her lip. 'Please, Heath, not tonight. I'm tired and I . . .' Her voice faded as she looked into his lean and hungry face.

'Are you? Or are you just making excuses because you're afraid?' Taking her key from her resistless hands, he opened the door of her room and led her inside. He closed the door behind them, but the room was flooded by moonlight and he didn't bother to turn on the light. Zara leant against the wall, time seeming to stand still as she waited for him to turn and take her in his arms, to gaze into her wide, staring eyes for a long moment, and then to breathe her name against her lips before he kissed her in fierce, urgent need, his body pressing against hers as passion rose like a volcano between them.

For a few moments Zara was so overwhelmed by the strength of his embrace that she succumbed to it completely, his arrant masculinity dominating her senses until she drowned in sensuality, lost to everything but his kiss. It was only when his lips left hers to kiss her eyes, her cheek, her neck, and his hands began to move over her, that Zara regained some fraction of rational thought and made a movement of protest, putting her hands against his chest and trying to push him away.

But he said, 'Yes,' fiercely and pulled her close to him, his arms holding her against the thrusting hardness of his body. 'I want you, Zara,' he said urgently, his lips hot on the skin of her throat. 'I want to take you to bed and make love to you. To look at your lovely body and feel your skin against mine. I want ...'

'Stop it! Get away from me!' With a strength magnified by anger, Zara shook herself free and pushed him violently away. Her hand went to the light switch and she clicked it on, chasing away the soft shadows of moonlight in its harsh glare.

Heath stood a couple of feet away from her, his hands doubled into white-knuckled fists, his square jaw thrust forward angrily as he glared at her. 'Now what?' he demanded tersely.

'I told you I didn't want this. I'm tired and I ...'

'No, you're not. And you want it as much as I do. But every time I kiss you you start to respond and then fight me off.'

'It's because you go too fast for me. You don't give me time to—to ...'

'Rubbish!' Stepping forward, Heath put his hand under her jaw, lifting her head up so that he could look down into her face. 'You like it when I kiss you. Don't you?' She didn't answer, so he pressed his mouth against hers forcefully, holding her prisoner under his lips. 'Don't you?' he insisted again.

Slowly Zara opened her eyes, unwilling to admit even that much, so she stayed silent, looking up at him resentfully.

'Yes,' Heath said softly, his gaze fixed intently on her face, 'your eyes give you away. You can't disguise the need in them any more than I can. You have such beautiful, expressive eyes, Zara. I always did love your eyes, and they were one of the first things that attracted me to you all those years ago.' He felt her stiffen and frowned down into her face. 'Now what did I say to make you angry, I wonder?'

Scenting danger, she moved away from him into the middle of the room so that he couldn't see her face. 'I'm not angry. But I—yes, I suppose I am a little afraid of you.'

Coming up behind her, Heath put his hands on her bare shoulders. 'You have no need to be.'

'Don't I?' She gave a shaky laugh. 'You're quite a fast worker, you know.'

He moved his hands down her arms, gently stroking them as he said, 'If you're so afraid of me, why did you ask me to come along on this trip?'

Thinking fast, and trying to ignore the sensuality of his touch, Zara answered jerkily, 'You said—you said you wanted us to get to know each other again. So I thought that—that this might be a good opportunity. But I can't . . . I don't . . .' Stepping away from him, she was able to think straight and said, 'I'm not ready to commit myself yet, Heath.' She looked at him pleadingly. 'You do understand?'

'No, not entirely. Is it just me you're afraid of—or all men?' He came nearer and stood looking down at her intently. 'Did you—commit yourself, as you put it—to Richard, for example?' Zara went to turn away, but he caught her arm. 'Well? Did you?' he demanded.

She looked angrily at his hand on her arm and opened her mouth to tell him to mind his own business, but his face was so urgently intense that the words died and she slowly shook her head. 'No,' she admitted dully.

Slowly Heath drew her to him. 'Or anyone else—since your marriage?'

'Please, Heath, I really don't want to talk about this. I . . .'

'But we must,' he insisted. 'Can't you see that? How can we ever get close to each other when you shrink away every time I touch you? But if you tell me why you're afraid then maybe we'll be able to work something out. At the very least, I'll understand why.' Putting a finger under her chin, he tilted her head so she had to look at him. 'So tell me, Zara—has there been anyone else since your husband?'

Her eyes shadowed and grew dark. There was no way she was going to tell him the whole truth, but some of it wouldn't matter—and it would gain time which was what she needed. So, her voice husky, she moved away from him and said, 'I tried. More than once. I—I was pretty desperate afterwards, you see. But—but it just never worked out. It was never right. And I couldn't—I couldn't *feel* anything.'

'Oh, my poor sweetheart!' Coming behind her again, Heath put his arms round her waist and held her against him. 'Was it so bad—with your husband?'

Zara stiffened and her voice grew bitter. 'Yes, it was bad,' she answered shortly. Her voice broke and suddenly she was telling him far more than she had ever intended. 'It was hell. Every time he touched me it was hell! I wanted to curl up and die.' She began to shake uncontrollably, her eyes wide and staring as she remembered.

'It's all right. Zara darling, it's all right.' Putting his arms round her, Heath turned her to face him and held her trembling body close, murmuring words of comfort and endearment.

Zara let the words roll over her, the tone of his voice and the strength of his arms creating a circle of protectiveness around her, a haven in which she could hide and feel safe. She had never spoken of what she had gone through before, had always kept it bottled up inside, and it had come as an emotional shock to speak of it now—and to Heath of all men. But although her body trembled in genuine distress, Zara didn't cry. She hadn't cried for a long, long time, not since Heath had deserted her. All that Christopher did to hurt her afterwards she had accepted with stoic fortitude, an attitude that had enraged Christopher and driven him to hurt her even more, to make her cry out in pain if nothing else. But she had never cried, even then, because nothing Christopher could do to her had hurt as much as Heath's abandonment. She had loved him so much. So much.

The trembling gradually stopped and she stood still and quiet in his arms. He was stroking her gently, like a child, but somehow, unconsciously, his touch subtly changed and they both became sexually aware of each other again. His hands were no longer soothing, instead becoming softly insinuating, sending a thrill of sensuality licking through her veins. Immediately Zara tried to move away, but Heath held her still. 'Don't be afraid,' he said softly. 'Don't ever be afraid of me.' He turned off the light and kissed her gently, first on her closed eyelids, then along her cheekbone, down to her chin and neck.

That was all right, Zara could stand that, she could even stand it when he nibbled her ear and moved on to explore her mouth with his tongue. But when his hands went to the thin straps of her dress and began to pull them down, she began to quiver again, making a sound of protest under his mouth.

'No, stand still. I'm not going to hurt you.'

His insistent hands went on pulling at the straps until the dress slipped down to her waist. Zara closed her eyes tightly but knew he was looking at her. 'You're beautiful,' Heath said softly. 'So lovely.'

She gasped as his hands began to explore her and she instinctively shrank away from his touch. But Heath persisted, his sensitive fingers handling her gently, his touch feather-light as he stroked and caressed her. All the while he gently kissed her face, murmuring endearments as he did so, telling her to relax, to take it easy. The nerves in her breasts came alive as he touched her. She could feel no other part of her body, only there. Her nipples felt as if they were on fire with heat and her breasts swollen and heavy. Where he fondled her they tingled, sending sparks of unbearable yearning seething through her body.

Sudden desire overcame her and she threw back her head, moaning as her nipples hardened and her breasts thrust towards him. Her breath came in short, gasping bursts as Heath went on caressing her, his touch firmer now that he knew she was aroused. And presently he put his hands on her arms, holding her still as he bent to kiss her breasts.

'No!' At first she tried to struggle, but his grip tightened, his fingers like steel bands that held her prisoner as he kissed her. His lips drove her mad, sucking and pulling at her already sensitive nipples until she cried out, unable to take any more, her body craving fulfilment, craving love.

When she began to writhe, Heath straightened up and held her close, her head on his shoulder. Zara stood trembling in his arms, her body so heated that she could taste her own sweat on her lips. 'You're a beautiful, sexual woman, Zara,' Heath said softly in her ear. 'You were made for love. And you want to be loved, don't you?' She stiffened a little, but he stood away from her and then turned her so that she could see her reflection in the full-length mirror on the wall.

The moon was still out and she could see herself quite clearly in its soft silver light. The moon accentuated the fine angles of her taut face, her eyes

wide and dark with need and her lips still parted in
desire. Her hair was a dishevelled halo around her
head, little tendrils of it clinging to her damp face. She
could see, too, the soft curve of her breasts, firm and
proud with the velvet elasticity of youth, the nipples
dark roses that were still hard from Heath's caresses.

'You see?' he said huskily as he came behind her and
put his hands on her shoulders. 'You're ripe for love,
Zara.' Putting his hands under her arms, he cupped her
breasts and began to caress them again. 'Open your
eyes,' he ordered, his own on her reflection in the
mirror.

'I—I can't.'

'Yes, you can. Open them, my darling. Look in the
mirror. Watch.' Slowly, reluctantly she obeyed him,
her eyes going to his hands as he began to fondle her
again. It was the most sexual experience she had ever
known—to stand and watch him touch her half-naked
body, to see the skilled way he caressed her to give the
maximum of pleasure. And to himself as well, for she
could feel the growing tension in his body as she leaned
back against him, her hips moving in voluptuous,
aching frustration and need.

Inadvertently his fingers tightened on her in
passion, but it acted like a warning bell in Zara's mind
and she jerked free of his hold, quickly pulling her dress
back on her shoulders.

Heath automatically reached out for her, but then
drew back. He smiled ruefully. 'Sorry—I'm afraid I
got a little carried away. You all right? I didn't hurt
you, did I?'

'No. But—but I think you'd better go.'

'All right.' Coming over to her, he put his arms

round her waist. 'Well, at least you didn't shrink away this time, so maybe we're getting somewhere.' He kissed her on the tip of her nose, smiling down at her. 'Maybe you even liked what we did tonight?'

'M-maybe.' He raised a quizzical eybrow so that she flushed and admitted, 'You know I did.'

'Yes.' Picking up her hand, Heath kissed her fingers. 'But it's good to hear you say it. Good to know that you're beginning to trust me.'

'Trust you?' Suddenly reality came flooding back and she wanted to strike out at him for his unbearable self-confidence, to tell him just what a fool she was making of him. But it was too soon for that, she must wait and hold him at arm's length a little longer. So instead she yawned and then laughed. 'Oh, I'm sorry. I think the time difference has suddenly hit me. I can hardly keep my eyes open!'

'Go to bed, then, sweetheart. I'll see you tomorrow.' Heath grinned. 'Unless of course you'd like me to put you to bed.'

Zara's breath caught, but she laughed shakily and said, 'Thanks, but I think I'd better manage that for myself.'

'For tonight anyway,' he said thickly. 'Maybe soon you'll realise you can trust me completely.' He gave her one last brief kiss of passion, then went to the door, making sure no one was outside before he said goodnight and finally left her alone.

Zara didn't sleep at all well that night, lying awake almost until dawn, staring at the dying moonlight patterns on the ceiling, her body still hot and filled with the fierce ache of frustration. She had breakfast sent up to her room and joined the others just as they were due to leave the hotel. Heath looked up eagerly when she arrived, but Zara only gave him a brief nod before putting on a pair of dark glasses which served the double purpose of hiding the dark shadows around her eyes and her feelings from Heath.

He had hired a couple of jeeps with striped sun awnings and they drove to a more deserted area of the beach where the photographer decided on what shots he wanted. It took quite a time to set everything up, the photographer wanting to get the light and distances right, but the team all worked well together and there was very little Zara could do to help. After watching for a while she went to sit with the other girls in the shade of a palm tree and asked them what they thought of the clothes they were to model. They were enthusiastic and all talked clothes for some time while Heath and the assistant helped to set up the photographer's equipment. Perhaps inevitably one of the girls said to Zara, 'I heard a rumour that you run the Panache company. But surely you're much too young?'

Zara laughed easily. 'Of course I don't run it. I just work there.'

'How about Heath?' Gemma, the girl who had been trying to attract him the night before, asked. 'Is he your boy-friend?'

'Why, no.' Zara looked at the girl under her lashes, scenting an opportunity to keep Heath out of her hair. 'No, I just know him from business meetings over this advertising campaign.'

'He works for the Masterads agency, doesn't he?'

'Not only works for it but owns it. In fact, you could

almost say that Heath Masterson *is* Masterads,' Zara emphasised.

'Really? He owns his own agency? And he's so macho too. I haven't met a man like him in ages.' Gemma looked at Zara. 'Are you making a play for him?'

Zara smiled slightly and shook her head. 'No, I have other—interests.'

'You won't mind, then, if I try to get to know him? Only he seems rather attracted to you.'

'Of course I don't mind. I wish you luck. And I'm sure you're mistaken. Like I said, he's just a business colleague, that's all.'

The photographer called the models over soon after and Zara strolled across to watch, deliberately standing next to the hairdresser so that Heath wouldn't have a chance to talk to her alone. But he came over anyway. He was wearing just a pale blue tee-shirt and darker blue, very short shorts, his strong legs already tanned, and his feet bare. Zara felt a tightening in her throat and could hardly answer him when he asked her whether she had got over her jet-lag.

'I suppose so. Although I—I didn't sleep very well.'

'Didn't you? Nor did I, as a matter of fact. Perhaps it's the change in temperature,' he added meaningly.

Zara gave him a quick look but then moved over to discuss the first change of swimwear for the models. They all worked more or less solidly all morning, but towards noon it got very hot and while the models were posing Zara decided to go in for a swim. She was wearing one of the Panache beach outfits herself; a pale orange one-piece swimsuit cut high at the sides to make the legs look longer and with an elongated diamond shape cut out of the front. Over it Zara wore a matching very long silky shirt, belted loosely at the hips, and her hair she had tied back in a plait with a twisted head band of the same orange material to complete the outfit.

Dropping the shirt on to the sand, she ran across the last few yards of beach and into the sea, beginning to swim as soon as she was in deep enough. The water felt cool and clean and beautiful. Lying on her back, Zara kicked her leg up in the air and watched the drops fly off in a thousand rainbow prisms reflected in the sunlight. She laughed, happy in her game, then turned to do a fast crawl out to a raft anchored in the bay, swam round it and back to the beach. She was still laughing happily as she ran out of the sea, drops of water clinging to her glistening body, and for a moment she wasn't aware that the photographer had walked down the beach and was snapping her as she ran towards him.

Catching sight of him, she laughed protestingly, but as she turned away saw that Heath, too, was watching her. She stopped, taken aback by the fierce flame of desire in his face, a desire that he made no attempt to hide. He began to walk towards her and she turned, like a bird ready to take flight, but he said. 'Wait,' in a strange harsh kind of voice which held her still.

Coming up to her, he put a hand on her arm, his eyes gazing so hungrily down into her face that she knew he was going to kiss her, right there in front of them all. Quickly she shook some water at him, splashing his face. 'Why don't you go in? The water's great.'

Heath blinked, then slowly grinned. 'Okay, why not?'

He put up his arms to pull off his shirt and Zara took the opportunity to call out and beckon the others. 'Come on! Come for a swim.'

They were all so hot that they didn't need any more encouragement to run and join them, only the photographer heroically staying on the beach to guard his equipment. Heath's mouth twisted wryly when he saw what was happening, but Gemma ran up and grabbed his hand, pulling him into the sea so that he had no chance to say anything. After their swim they had lunch at a beach restaurant and then drove to the harbour where they took some more shots with the big ocean liners in the background, and some shots of the nearby straw market. Heath tried to get Zara alone several times, but among so many people she was able to be with someone all the time and as Gemma was trying to get Heath alone she didn't have too much difficulty.

When they got back to the hotel Zara went to see the receptionist and then announced to the others that she had managed to get tickets for them all to go and see the show at the Casino Theatre that evening. Heath frowned, but there was nothing he could do about it, especially as Gemma went up to him, put her arm familiarly through his, and said, 'Isn't that great? And we'll be able to go to the casino and play the tables afterwards. My favourite game is roulette. What's yours?'

Leaving Heath to try and extricate himself, Zara ran up to her room and put a call through to her stockbroker in London. 'Have you got the Masterad shares for me yet?' she asked him.

'It's all going smoothly. We hope to finalise the deal

tomorrow or the day after.'

'Can't you be more specific?' Zara asked impatiently. 'I don't want to have to stay here longer than
necessary.'

'I'm sorry, Miss Layston, but this isn't the kind of
deal we can push. It has to be done with—er—tact.'

'Well, just let me know the minute the deal's
complete, won't you?'

She had hardly put the phone down when it rang
again. For a moment she hesitated, but then picked up
the receiver in case it was a call from her office in
London. But, as she had feared, it was Heath.

'How about ducking out on the others and having
dinner alone together tonight?' he suggested.

'But I've got tickets for the show. And everyone says
that it's very good, really spectacular.'

'And I suppose you really want to see it?'

'Well, yes, I do.'

'Are you trying to avoid me again, Zara?'

She laughed lightly. 'Of course not.'

'Then promise to spend the day with me tomorrow.'

'I can't do that—the photographer might need us to
help him.'

'He can manage perfectly well without us and you
know it.'

In the end she had to agree to have dinner with him
the next evening and just kept her fingers crossed that
she would be able to make a last-minute excuse to get
out of it. But she knew that Heath, having made what
he felt to be some progress with her, was impatient to
be alone with her again and wouldn't for long be
fobbed off with any more excuses. And if he tried to
make love to her again—Zara's heart froze—maybe

this time he wouldn't be willing to stop.

But at least she was safe and could relax tonight. They had a good dinner at a restaurant on the main island, a couple of them ordering seafood and the others experimenting with Caribbean dishes. The show too, was extremely good, the most spectacular that Zara had ever seen outside Paris. Afterwards they all went into the casino where the fruit-machine handles were red-hot from the tourists who continuously poured silver dollars into them. Gemma immediately got hold of Heath and led him towards the roulette tables, followed by the others who played or stood and watched. Zara found herself next to the photographer and asked him how much longer he would need to take the rest of the photographs.

'Another day should do it. I thought of taking a few in the old town and some in the Botanical Gardens. If that's okay with you?'

'Yes, of course, that's fine. I'll book seats on a plane the day after tomorrow, then.'

'Make it an afternoon plane, will you? I'm having the films I've taken developed at a local studio overnight and I want to see how they come out before we leave.'

Zara nodded and went on chatting to him for a while, but when she saw that Heath's attention was held by Gemma, she slipped away and went up to bed.

Disaster hit them the next morning. The phone rang while Zara was dressing and the photographer told her that both his assistant and the other model had been taken ill in the night. 'They're sending for a doctor,' he told her, 'but it sounds very much like food poisoning. If you remember they both had the lobster last night.'

'Oh no! What are we going to do? Can you manage with only one model?'

'Not really. We'd better meet for breakfast and discuss it. I've already phoned Heath.'

Zara went along to visit the invalids and ordered a nurse to look after them, then joined the other four for breakfast. 'Hallo. What a terrible thing to happen,' she greeted them. 'I suppose we'll just have to wait until they're better before we can finish the assignment.'

Heath and the two girls began to agree with her, but the photographer, who had been looking through a large brown envelope of photographs, suddenly sat up straight and said, 'No, we won't.'

They turned to him in surprise as he handed over a few of the photographs. They were of Zara running out of the sea, the sun kissing her body, and flying droplets of water like sprays of diamonds caught for ever by the camera. There was another photograph, too—of her and Heath when he had come up to her and put his hand on her arm. It was all there in their faces; Heath's sharp and tense with desire, hers vulnerable and afraid. But there was awareness there, too, in her parted lips and wide eyes. Zara grew still as she looked at the photograph, then slowly lifted her head to look at Heath. His eyes glanced at her for a moment, then he leaned across and took the photo from her hands to look at it himself.

'You see? You're a natural!' the photographer was saying excitedly. 'You could easily model some of the clothes for us today. And if we need a man in any of the shots we can use Heath as a stand-in.' He went on talking persuasively, but Zara's eyes had met Heath's over the photograph and suddenly it seemed as if there were no one else in the place. The crowded hotel dining-room was still and empty, there was no one but the two of them in the hotel, on the island, in the world. And because she wasn't listening properly, Zara murmured yes when the photographer asked her something and when she slowly came back to reality found that she had agreed to model for him.

'Oh, I didn't mean ...'

But she was given no time to protest and soon found herself having her hair done and posing for shots while the photographer instructed her what to do. She did as he asked, leaning up against walls and trees, sitting in the driving-seat of one of the jeeps and always smiling, smiling, but all the time feeling in a numb kind of haze. A few times she had to pose with Heath, often with his arm around her waist or shoulders, and only then her senses came alive again as he touched her.

Because she was inexperienced it took longer and the sun was already beginning to go down when the photographer said he wanted to go back to the beach. 'The shots I took of the bikini didn't come out too well. I want to take them again.'

So they drove back to Paradise Beach and Zara put on a pale green bikini with halter straps. He shot her alone first, running along the beach with the sunset behind her, standing on the edge of a breakwater, silhouetted against the horizon, and listening to a conch shell. But then he wanted Heath to strip off his shirt and pose with her in just their swimsuits. Her heart beating crazily, Zara stood beside him, but the photographer said impatiently, 'No, no, put some life into it. Face him and lean against him. Yes, that's better.'

Heath put his hands on her waist, looking at her quizzically as she leaned against his chest. His skin felt hot and smooth to her touch, the tiny hairs glowing in the deep orange flare of the sunset.

'Now put your left arm round his neck, and your right on his chest—that's it. Now look at him, please.'

Zara slowly obeyed him, lifting her head until her eyes, shy and uncertain, met Heath's. His gaze held hers for a long moment and then, completely oblivious of the camera, he bent his head to kiss her. And as her mouth yielded under the pressure of his she acknowledged the truth that she had known in her heart all that day—that she had fallen in love with Heath all over again.

CHAPTER SEVEN

TEARING herself free from Heath's embrace, Zara turned and ran back up the beach, snapping out to the photographer, 'I've had enough. I'm going back to the hotel.'

'All right. The sun's almost set anyway.'

He began to pack his equipment away while Zara quickly put on slacks and a shirt and went over to sit in the back seat of one of the jeeps to wait, staring down at her hands gripped together in her lap.

Heath followed up the beach more slowly and pulled on his shirt, then walked over to the jeep.

Fully aware of him although she didn't look round, Zara burst out, 'Go away! Damn you, Heath, just go away and leave me alone!'

'Before you've even heard what I have to say?'

'There's nothing you can possibly say that I want to hear.'

Heath's face hardened. 'But maybe I want to say it all the same.'

But he had no chance to, because the make-up girl came over to load some clothes into the jeep just as the photographer called Heath over to give him a hand. He went reluctantly and had to drive the other jeep back to the hotel through the rapidly darkening night, so Zara was at least spared that. And when they arrived she just left the others and fled to her room, locking the door and pushing the bolt across as if all the

151

devils in hell were behind her.

For a moment she leant against the door in relief, but then remembered the balcony and hurried to close those doors too. Admittedly there was a chest-high wall which curved outwards between the two balconies, but Zara had no doubt that Heath could climb round that easily if he was determined enough, even though they were on the fifth floor! Agitatedly she closed the blinds, then ran to the phone, just as someone rapped on her door. She stood frozen, clutching the receiver tightly, instinctively knowing it was Heath and afraid to make a sound, stupidly hoping that he would think she wasn't there and go away.

But he rapped on the door again and called, 'Zara, I know you're in there. What's the point in . . .'

His voice broke off and she guessed that some other people must have come up in the lift. In her ear she heard the switchboard operator's voice asking her what she wanted, but she didn't answer, afraid Heath might hear her voice. But he didn't knock again and her straining ears heard his own door slam shut. Only then did she speak hurriedly into the phone. 'Operator? Yes, I'm sorry, I do want to make a call. Would you put me through to the airport, please?' After what seemed to her impatient mind like hours, she was at last put through and was able to book a seat on a plane flying to Miami that evening, which would connect with another going to London a couple of hours later.

Thank goodness! Zara heaved a sigh of relief and put the receiver down. Which was a mistake, because it immediately rang. Tension flooded through her, so strongly that it was as if she could feel it coming through the wall from Heath's room. Slowly she picked up the receiver, but didn't speak.

'Zara?' He said her name urgently, then added quickly, 'Don't put the phone down. I just want to see you for a few minutes, that's all. We can ...'

But Zara cut him off, her hand trembling, then immediately got through to the receptionist to ask if there were any messages for her.

'Yes, ma'am, there's a cable from England. Shall I have it sent up?'

'Please. As soon as possible.' While she was waiting Zara got out her suitcase and began to throw things in haphazardly, then belatedly remembered the two sick members of their team and rang the photographer to ask how they were. He reported that they were both much better and would be able to leave the following day.

'Oh, that's good news. Look, I'm sorry, but something has happened in England and I'll have to fly home ahead of you. But I'm sure you'll be able to manage. Tell the girls they can keep the clothes, will you? And thank them for all their hard work. And my thanks to you, of course. I'll look forward to seeing all the photos when you get back.' A knock sounded on the door, a much more gentle one this time. 'I'm sorry, I'll have to go. Look forward to seeing you back in London. 'Bye.'

Crossing over to the door, Zara took the precaution of saying, 'Who is it?' before she opened it.

'Cable for you, ma'am.'

The voice definitely wasn't Heath's, so she opened the door a fraction and saw a hotel boy outside with her cable in his hand. 'Just a moment.' Taking some money from her purse, Zara opened the door properly to give him the tip and take the cable. But as she went to close it again Heath came up behind the boy and held it firmly open as he pushed past her into the room, saying, 'Hallo, darling, have we got a cable? Who's it from, I wonder?'

Before she could do more than open her mouth to call the boy back, Heath had pushed the door closed. Then he held her against the wall, his eyes glinting down at her for a moment before he bent to kiss her.

It had all happened so suddenly that for a few moments she was unable to react, but then she began to struggle, knowing that if she succumbed to his kisses she would be lost. Heath's hands tightened on her and she thought he was going to use his strength to overpower her, to hold her prisoner while he did what he wanted. She struggled harder in a sudden panic of fear, and this time he lifted his head, although he still held her by the arms.

It was nearly dark in the room now, the sun's last dying embers of flame almost completely lost below the horizon. 'Zara,' Heath said softly. 'Zara, sweetheart.' And putting up his hand he began to caress her face gently.

'No, don't touch me!' Knocking his hand away, Zara reached out and switched on the lights, her angry, hate-filled eyes making Heath draw back in startled surprise. 'Get out of my room. Go on, get out!'

He stared at her, a growing frown between his eyes, but then he shook his head decisively. 'No, we have to talk. I'm getting tired of you behaving as if I'm some kind of ogre every time I come near you. We're going to talk this out here and now.'

Drawing her away from the door, he caught sight of

her partly-packed suitcase on the bed. 'Running away again, Zara?' he asked grimly.

'I can do anything I want! And I certainly don't want to listen to you. So you can just clear out of here before I . . .'

His jaw thrusting forward, Heath said tersely, 'Shut up! For once in your life you're going to sit down and listen!' And he pushed her down into a chair by the dressing-table. He stood looming over her, his clenched fists on his hips, and still dressed only in shorts and a sweat shirt, his muscular body hard with tension. 'I've been as patient as I know how to be with you,' he said forcefully. 'Okay, I know you had a tough time with your husband and it's put you off men. But you've had time to get over it.'

Glaring up at him, Zara said shortly, 'There are some things you never get over.'

But Heath dismissed that with an impatient wave of his hand. 'You're a grown woman, Zara—you must know that all men aren't the same. Just because you made one mistake it doesn't mean that you have to run away when a man wants to get close to you—wants to love you,' he added deliberately.

'That's all men ever want, all they ever think about! They think because they take you out a couple of times that they have the right to go to bed with you. But if you think . . .'

Putting his hands on the arms of her chair, Heath leaned forward angrily. 'Why don't you listen? I said love, not sex. Okay, sex is very much a part of love. A physical demonstration of it, if you like. But what I feel for you goes much deeper than that. And you feel it, too. You realised it back there on the beach. But like the coward you are, you're trying to run away from it.'

Zara sat hunched in the chair, trying to withdraw into herself, to keep as far away from Heath as possible. She looked up at him, her features a mixture of fright and resentment. 'I don't want to love you. I don't want to get hurt again.'

'You *won't* get hurt. I've told you, I'm not like your husband. I want to love and cherish you, not hurt you.'

But Zara had been thinking about him, not Christopher. A wintry smile flicked across her face. Men were so conceited; did he really think she would ever forget or forgive the way he had let her down?

But Heath was saying persuasively, 'Zara, I *know* we can be happy together. I love you very much, darling. I want to marry you. I want to teach you how wonderful love can be.' He lifted one hand to touch her and then stopped himself, but said urgently, 'And you love me too, don't you? *Don't you, Zara?* You can't deny it— even to yourself, not any more.'

For a long moment she didn't answer, but then she nodded tiredly. 'Yes. I'm in love with you—God help me.' And thought bitterly: And that's why I have to destroy you, destroy you utterly and quickly, so you never have the power to hurt me again as you did before.

'Darling!' Heath's face lit with pleasure and he laughed at her expression. 'Don't look so unhappy.' Putting his hands on her waist, he drew her to her feet. 'You won't ever regret it, I promise you.' Holding her in his arms, he said softly, 'I'm going to teach you not to be afraid any more. Soon you'll know that going to bed with the person you love is the most wonderful experience you can ever imagine.'

He kissed her face gently and she didn't try to fight him, but she didn't close her eyes, just stood in withdrawn animosity, waiting for him to go.

Heath laughed again. 'Oh, my poor darling, you're so angry, aren't you? Is it with me—or with yourself for falling in love with me? But I'm going to make you happy, I swear it. You enjoyed what we did the other night, you know you did. And whether you like it or not your body is crying out to be loved. You try to fight it but you're as hungry for it as I am. That's why you tremble whenever I kiss you and why you're afraid to let me caress you in case your body takes over from your head.' He smiled tenderly down at her. 'But now you don't stand a chance, my love, because I have your heart on my side too.' He kissed her eyes, her cheeks, her throat, slowly, luxuriously, as if he already possessed her, taking it for granted that because she had admitted that she loved him she was ready to do what he wanted, agree to anything he wanted to do.

Holding her close, he said, 'Zara, we need time. Time alone together, away from London and work and people. Even just a few days could make all the difference in the world for us. We need to be alone so that you can get used to being touched and kissed, can learn to trust me completely. And what better place than here?'

Zara drew back, staring at him. 'You mean you want to stay on here?'

'Yes, to give ourselves a few days after the others go back.'

'So that I can get used to you—handling me?' she said harshly. 'It's out of the question, I can't spare the time.'

'Then *make* time,' Heath said fiercely. 'Zara, we need to be together, and it has to be *now*.'

'Are you ordering me to stay?' she demanded haughtily.

'Yes, if that's the only thing that you'll listen to.' Putting his hands on her shouders, he said earnestly, 'Zara, you owe it to yourself—and you owe it to me for what happened in the past.'

She shook him off violently at that. 'I don't owe you a thing!'

'All right—forget the past, then. Maybe it is better to start clean. But you *have* to give us a chance, Zara.'

For a minute she glared at him antagonistically, then suddenly capitulated. 'Oh, all right—but only for a few days. Then I'm going home.'

He gave a crooked kind of grin. 'Such enthusiasm! Anyone would think I was asking you to submit to torture!' His face changed. 'I'm sorry. Maybe it once was torture for you, but it won't be any more, I promise.'

Zara looked at him, nodded and turned away to sit on the bed. 'I'll—I'll have to send a cable to London; tell them not to meet me tomorrow.'

'Okay. Then we'll change and start by going out to dinner, just the two of us.' He moved to go but then stopped. 'You do mean it, don't you? You won't try to run away again.' She shook her head but that didn't satisfy him. Coming over, he made her look at him and said, 'Say it, Zara. Promise me that you'll stay.'

'Yes, all right, I promise.'

'Good girl.' He kissed her on the nose and straightened up. 'See you in how long—an hour?'

She nodded. 'Yes, all right. In an hour.'

When he had gone Zara sat looking down at her hands twisted together in her lap for some time, then remembered her cable and went to pick it up from where it had fallen, forgotten, on the floor. It said simply, 'Maximum shares now bought. You own fifty-five per cent.' So—she had what she had been waiting for. Without even bothering to think about it, she changed into a travelling outfit, packed the rest of her things, then turned on the shower in the bathroom that backed on to Heath's room to cover the noise of her door opening, and left the hotel as quickly as she could. In less than two hours she was arriving in Miami and in four was on another plane on her way home to London.

Heath was going to be very, very angry, especially when he found out that he was no longer in control of his own company. Of this Zara was fully aware, but she was a day ahead of him and could take adequate precautions. When the plane landed at Heathrow Airport she took a taxi directly to her office, arriving there at around midday. She hadn't slept very much on the plane, but the adrenalin of victory and excitement was flowing in her veins and she was fully alert.

The receptionist looked up from her desk as Zara entered the building and greeted her with a warm smile. 'Why, Miss Layston! We didn't expect you back until tomorrow. Did you enjoy your break—you look beautifully tanned.'

'Do I? Yes, I suppose it was quite a change.' She smiled at the girl and added casually, 'If anyone from Masterads comes to the office will you make sure that they're not allowed past your desk without phoning me first, please?'

Mac was in the outer office, leaning back in his

chair, his feet up on the desk and a mug of coffee in his hand as he read a newspaper. She walked in with a brisk, 'Hallo, Mac,' and he choked as the coffee went down the wrong way.

'Don't do that to me!' he spluttered. 'You're not supposed to be here. You're supposed to be in the Bahamas having an affair with Heath Master . . .' He stopped abruptly, realising what he was saying.

Zara looked at him sardonically. 'Am I indeed? I wonder how that rumour got around. You can make a coffee for me and bring it into my office while you fill me in on everything that's happened while I've been away. But get the porter of my apartment building on the line first, please.'

She went into her own office and Mac put the call through. Tersely, Zara instructed the porter not on any account to let Heath up to her flat in the future, her fear of Heath's reaction overcoming her usual regard for her privacy. If it aroused the curiosity of the porter and her colleagues it was just too bad.

Mac came in with her coffee and together they went through her in-tray, but Mac had been very efficient and there wasn't a lot to do, although she would have a busy schedule of meetings in the weeks ahead. When they had gone through the work Zara said, 'There's one extra letter I want typed. And I want you to do this yourself, Mac, and do two extra copies, one to go to our solicitor and the other to be put in the safe. I want the top copy also to be delivered by hand today. I did a draft of the letter on the plane.'

She handed a sheet of paper to him and Mac's eyes widened incredulously as he read it. 'My God, Zara, you can't do this!' he ejaculated.

'Why not?' she returned, her voice quite calm and cool.

'Because—because it's not ethical. You can't just turn round and tell Masterads you no longer want them to do any more work for us at this stage. It's gone too far. Think of all the work they've already done.'

'If you read the letter through you'll see that I've said that we will continue to use the Masterads agency so long as Heath Masterson is no longer associated with it.'

Mac looked at her aghast. 'But he *is* Masterads!'

'Rubbish! He's only a glorified salesman.'

'Zara——' Mac hesitated, then said firmly, 'Look, you can't let personal feelings influence you like this. You have no right to do this to the agency just because Heath has upset you in some way. You can't . . .'

Zara's green eyes narrowed dangerously. 'And just what right have you to tell me what I can or can't do, Mac?' she asked silkily.

Recognising the danger signals, he stood up. 'All right, I'll type the letter, but *please*, think about it. A lot of people are dependent on Masterads for work, you know. Especially as they've been taking on extra staff. This move you're making could ruin the agency.'

Zara already knew that, knew it full well, but she had given Heath the option of saving the agency if he himself got out—which choice he made was up to him. And being now a majority shareholder of Masterads she was in a position to see that no one else there suffered; she could always offer them jobs with Panache if Masterads folded.

Her secretary went away to type the letter, and Zara wasn't at all surprised when, about ten minutes later,

Colin Royle, the marketing manager, rang and asked if he could see her. 'Hi. Had a good holiday?' he asked heartily when he came in.

'I wasn't on holiday. You may remember I was working,' she pointed out.

'Oh yes, of course. Must have made a pleasant break, though.'

'Very pleasant,' Zara agreed. 'Did you want something specific, Colin?'

'Just to bring you up to date on the Game, Set and Match promotion. Everything's going along very well. Couldn't be better, in fact. We're all set to go in a month's time.' He looked at her expectantly but Zara didn't say anything. 'Er—I take it you got all the photographs you wanted for the swimwear? Everything went okay, did it?'

Leaning back in her chair, Zara looked at him and said calmly, 'How does it feel to be made of glass?'

Colin gave a wry grin. 'Meaning you can see right through me, I suppose?'

'Quite. And you're wasting your time. I knew Mac would be straight on to you, but you're not going to persuade me to change my mind.'

'I don't even know what it is I'm supposed to change your mind about. Mac just said I ought to get along here fast and reassure you about how good Masterads are being over the promotion. So what's going on?'

'I should be free at the end of the afternoon, we'll talk about it then.'

He had no choice but to agree and went away wondering what on earth was happening, leaving Zara free to phone the company solicitor and ask him to come round to see her as soon as he could. With a company as important as Panache, he was at her office within the hour and the two of them went through the letter she had written together with their contract with Masterads.

'Yes,' the solicitor agreed. 'This clause you had put in the contract giving you the right to back out if this Heath Masterson was no longer able to give your contract his personal attention, or if you no longer find his work up to the standard you require, gives you the right to dispense with them at any time.' He raised his eyebrows. 'I take it that you do have adequate reason for sending this?'

Zara nodded. 'Adequate enough.'

'By all means send it, then. The most they can do is to argue that you're mistaken, but I doubt very much if they would want to bring a lengthy court case against you.'

'That's what I thought,' she agreed. She signed her name firmly and gave the letter to Mac, telling him to take it round to Masterads himself and to be sure to get a signature for it. 'And Mac,' she added, 'when you get back I want you to make sure that Heath is never allowed into our offices—especially mine. Do you understand?'

'No,' Mac answered roundly. 'I don't understand what's got into you lately at all. But I'll do as you ask, of course.'

When he had gone Zara sat back with a small sigh, realising that there was no going back now. Not that she wanted to go back. All her work of the last weeks had been towards this end, and she could only be fiercely glad that Heath was going to learn what she really thought of him at last.

She went out for a sandwich but was too tense to eat, and strangely she still didn't feel at all sleepy even though she had been travelling all night. The adrenalin was still running too high, as was an almost fascinated apprehension about what Heath's reaction would be. That he would try to get to her, to attempt either to argue or to cajole her into changing her mind she was quite sure. But Zara had no intention of seeing Heath if she could possibly avoid it. She rather thought that bringing pressure to bear on him from a distance would be far more effective than a face-to-face confrontation. Glancing at her watch, she calculated that it would be several hours yet before he would be able to fly back to England and reach his office. Maybe he wouldn't even bother to go there today at all and so he might not read her letter until tomorrow morning. Whether or not he would try to contact her tonight after she had left him high and dry in Nassau, Zara didn't know. She toyed with the idea of asking a friend to spend the evening with her at her flat, just in case Heath came round, but decided that she would be safe enough with the porter to bar his way. Thinking about it, she suddenly felt sick of the whole thing and walked briskly back to the office to get on with some work.

It was just as well she had hurried. She had only been back in the office for about ten minutes when there was the noise of a commotion out in the reception area and then the door to Mac's office was thrown open and Heath burst in. He must have moved heaven and earth to have got back so soon after her. Jumping to his feet, Mac said, 'You can't go in there,' as Heath headed angrily towards Zara's door.

'Just try and stop me!' Heath snarled.

Mac gamely did try, and was pushed out of the way like a fly. 'Keep away from me or I'll knock your head off!' Heath threatened. He flung open the door of Zara's office, sending it flying back against the wall, and strode in, big and powerful and furiously angry.

Zara had been in the act of looking through a file of design drawings at her desk and had sat frozen from the first sound. But Heath stopped short on the other side of the desk, his eyes glaring at her murderously. 'You made a promise to stay in Nassau,' he reminded her savagely.

Zara's face was drawn but her voice was icy calm as she said, 'I'm under no obligation to keep promises to someone who doesn't keep them himself.'

'You bitch! You cowardly little bitch!' he shot at her. For a moment she wasn't sure whether he knew or not, but then he dragged the letter from his pocket and threw it on the desk. 'What the hell do you mean by this?'

Behind him Mac had come to the door. 'I told you that Miss Layston doesn't want to see you. You can make an appointment some other time and . . .'

Goaded beyond endurance, Heath turned round and took hold of Mac, propelling him into the outer office, then slamming the door behind him and locking it.

Zara got to her feet, her face white. 'How *dare* you throw my secretary out? Just who the hell do you think you are?'

'Right now I'm damn angry, so don't push it.' He glared at her, his face set with fury. 'I want an explanation for this.' And he jabbed at the letter lying on the desk.

'It's explanation enough. I no longer have any use for you or your agency. Now get out of here.'

Picking up the telephone receiver, Zara began to jab at the numbers for the security guard, but Heath lunged across and grabbed the receiver from her hand, then tore the wires from the socket. 'Now it's just you and me,' he said grimly.

Angry herself now, she threw the useless receiver at him and ran for the door, but he ducked and grabbed her arm, spinning her round to face him. 'Oh, no, you don't! You're not going to run away from me again.' And he took the key out of the lock and put it in his pocket. 'Now,' he said harshly, 'I want an explanation.'

'I should have thought that was obvious,' she retorted. 'I don't want you around.'

'Okay, so you're a craven-hearted little coward who's afraid even to take a chance on being in love,' Heath said savagely. 'But my God, you must be mad to go as far as wanting to get rid of my agency as well as me!'

'On the contrary,' Zara returned with cold anger, 'I know exactly what I'm doing.'

'Do you?' His grip tightened on her arm and he pulled her closer so that he was looking directly into her face. 'Why are you taking it out on me like this?' he demanded helplessly. 'All I ever wanted was to love you.' His jaw hardened. 'But maybe you can't help it at that. Maybe you have the kind of sadistic nature that makes you turn on everyone who loves you. Maybe that's why we never made it before—and possibly even why your husband turned against you. Is that the reason, Zara?' he jeered. 'Do you like hurting people?'

'No!' She shouted the word at him and tried to pull

free, but his hold was like a vice.

Someone banged on the door and Mac's voice shouted, 'Zara, are you all right?'

She went to shout back, but Heath put his hand over her mouth and called, 'Everything's fine. We're just having a private talk.'

The banging stopped and she glared at him as Heath took his hand away. 'Why don't you get out of here? There's nothing here for you. Not me, my money, or the fat contracts you were angling for.'

His eyes narrowed. 'So that's it, is it? You really think that all I wanted was your damn money.' He shook his head, his voice scathing. 'You couldn't be more wrong. I've always wanted you.'

Zara laughed harshly. 'Oh, I'll admit you put on a very good act, but do you really think I was fool enough to be taken in a second time? No, all I had to do was to dangle my golden hook in front of your eyes and you were too greedy to resist it. You walked straight into the trap I set for you.'

Heath's eyes became wary. 'Trap?'

'Yes, it's all been a set-up, right from the beginning. Do you really believe I would have even looked at your agency knowing you were the head of it? But I saw a way to get even with you and I took it. I even went out with you and put up with your disgusting kisses and the way you pawed me just so that I could ruin you once and for all. And now I have,' she ended triumphantly. 'You're finished! And finished for good—I'll make sure of that!'

Heath was staring at her, an unbelieving look in his eyes. 'And just what,' he said slowly, 'am I supposed to have done to you to turn you into such a vindictive little bitch?'

That made her flinch a little, but she answered angrily, 'As if you didn't know!' Her nostrils flared disgustedly. 'What's the point in going on pretending? We both know what kind of a swine you are. Only I wasn't rich then, was I? You couldn't clear out fast enough when I told you I loved you.' She had begun to shake and her hands were balled into tight fists. 'And then you came back and found I was successful, so you thought you could just crook your finger and I'd fall at your feet again. But not this time, mister. Oh no, not this time,' she finished bitterly, her voice catching in her throat.

His face white, Heath said tersely, 'Let's get this straight. Are you saying that it was I who broke us up all those years ago?' Zara opened her mouth to make a scornful reply, but Heath shook his head in perplexity and said, 'Because I was led to believe that it was you who'd changed your mind.'

Zara laughed in his face. 'I have to hand it to you, Heath, you just don't give up. But you're wasting your breath with your lies. Either you resign from Masterads or I'll drop the agency altogether.'

Heath's face hardened, grew angry again. 'And I'll sue you for breach of contract.'

She gave him a cold smile. 'Such a shame, but I'm not in breach of the contract. Don't you remember the clause that says if we don't get your personal attention or we're not satisfied with your work, the contract is void?'

'You have no reason to be dissatisfied with my work. And I've certainly given *you* my personal attention,' he added sardonically.

A flush of colour came into her pale cheeks as she said, 'But that's the clause I'm going to use.'

'By God, I'll fight you, then! I'm not going to have you slander my professional reputation just because of some crazy personal vendetta. I've done my best work for you and you know it,' he snapped, his voice growing hot and angry again.

Unconsciously putting the desk between them, Zara played her trump card. 'You're mistaken. I'm not breaking the contract because of the standard of your work—but because your services will shortly no longer be available to us.'

'And just what's that supposed to mean?' Heath demanded.

'It means that an extraordinary general meeting of Masterads' shareholders will shortly be called in which you will not only be voted off the board of directors but you will also be called on to resign from the agency.'

His face had gone very white. 'What the hell do you mean?'

'It means that I've been buying up the shares in your company and now have a fifty-five per cent holding. I control Masterads now, not you. And you're out.'

'My God!' He stared at her, unable to speak for a moment, then took a swift stride across the room and grabbed her. 'Why, you little . . .' Infuriated beyond measure, he shook her, his eyes murderous, and for a few terrified seconds Zara was really afraid, but then he pushed her violently away from him, even in his fury unable to hurt her. Savagely he said, 'And you'd do all this, go to all those lengths, just because you believed that I let you down seven years ago? And to think I really wanted to marry you! A mad, cruel-hearted little viper who . . .'

Shaking with rage herself, Zara shouted, 'Is that all it was to you? Just a let-down? My God, don't you know what you did to me? *I loved you.* I was willing to give up everything for you: my family, my home, my education, my—my virginity. They were all yours for the taking. But as soon as I said I was in love with you you took fright and left without even saying goodbye.' A great shudder ran through her. 'I waited and waited for you to phone or write. I couldn't bear to go to school or to go out in case I missed your call.' She laughed, a hard unnatural laugh that spoke volumes in itself. 'What a poor besotted fool I was, wasn't I? As if you ever really cared. But I cared—God, how I loved you! I didn't want to go on living without you. And then, when I knew it was hopeless, nothing semed to matter any more, so I married Christopher because he at least wanted me.' She bit her lip for a moment and held on to the edge of the desk, her nails digging into the wood. 'Can you imagine what it's like to go to bed with a man when you're in love with someone else? Your mind fights against it and your body won't react. You just lie there rigidly, praying for it soon to be over. I tried to pretend, but I couldn't, and—and after a while I couldn't stand it any more. Then Christopher forced me to tell him about you. And when he realised that every time he kissed me I was comparing him to you, and every time he touched me I was wishing it was you, then he became cruel and began to force me to do what he wanted. And the terrible thing is that he started to *enjoy* hurting me.' Zara's voice had slowed into dull sadness as she spoke, but now she looked at Heath bitterly. 'So you see, you didn't just clear out, you left a trail of unhappiness behind you that ruined our lives for years. And that's why I've ruined you, because I've hated you for a very, very long time.'

Heath's face had gone very pale beneath his tan. 'Then I can only feel sorry for you, Zara. Because that isn't the way it happened at all. I was in love with you, too, and I was all set to take you to America with me. But when I rang you the day after I saw you last your father answered the phone when I called. He told me that you were only eighteen—which came as a pretty shattering blow. He also told me that you were still at school and the plans you had to go to university. He said that to throw all that away on someone you hardly knew was absurd and that you'd talked it over with your parents and realised this. And that you'd decided to break it off. I had to accept that, but when he asked me not to contact you again I refused because I was so in love with you. I said that I wanted to write to you while I was away in the hope that we could get together again when you were older. So I tried to phone you two or three times before I left, but either your sister or one of your parents said you'd gone out with your boyfriend. Then I wrote from America but never got any reply to my letters. And when I came home to England on holiday the following year I tried to get in touch with you, but I found out that you were married.' His voice grew heavy. 'So the only conclusion I could reach was that it had just been an infatuation with you, a romantic adventure, but that you'd never really loved me at all.'

Zara's eyes were wide as she stared at him, every speck of colour drained from her face. 'You're lying,' she said faintly. 'It can't be true.'

Heath looked at her pityingly. 'Why don't you ask your parents? Perhaps by now they'll be willing to tell you the truth.'

Their eyes met for a long moment, Heath's scornful, Zara's blank with shock, then he turned, unlocked the door and strode out of the office.

CHAPTER EIGHT

Mac was waiting just outside and watched Heath go warily, then hurried into her room. 'Zara, are you all right?'

She stared past him, not even hearing or seeing him. Heath's words kept whirling round and round in her brain, slow realisation that they could be true a living nightmare. Part of her mind fought against it, because if it were so then she had done the most terrible thing. But it couldn't be true, she had received no letters from him. Unless her parents had intercepted those, too. If it were true then . . . The sheer horror of all those wasted years burst in her brain and she dropped to the floor at Mac's feet.

They wouldn't let her go home alone. They all fussed over her and Mac made one of the girls go back to the flat with her and spend the night there. He also wanted to call a doctor, but this Zara had the strength to refuse, saying it was probably just jet-lag and lack of sleep catching up with her. No one believed her, but they were kind and pretended to for her sake. But she was glad to get home, glad to go to bed and lie there in the darkened room, her mind a conflicting turmoil of doubt and fear.

In the morning she got up early and sat by the window looking out over the park, waiting for the other girl to waken. When she did, Zara got her some breakfast, thanked her for staying and said that she didn't think she would go into the office that day.

'I'll stay with you, then,' the girl offered.

'Oh no, I'm fine now. Really. And besides, I've decided to go and spend the day with my parents.'

The girl's brow cleared. 'That's all right, then.' But then she frowned. 'Will you drive yourself or shall I tell them to send the car round to take you?'

Zara nodded and to the girl's relief said, 'Please. I never did get round to learning to drive.'

So she travelled out to her parents' home about forty miles away in the company car, her face still very pale and a desperate look in her eyes. Her mother answered the door and exclaimed in surprise, 'Why, Zara! We didn't expect to see you today.' She glanced past her daughter to the car. 'Were you passing?'

'No. I—I wanted to see you.'

Looking at her face, Mrs Layston went a little pale herself. She led the way into the sitting-room and said nervously, 'Is there anything wrong?'

'I don't know. I've come to you to find out.' Zara hesitated, finding it difficult to talk to her mother. She had been able to talk and confide in her once, but not for a very long time now, not since the terrible rows when she had wanted to go away with Heath, and afterwards when she had wanted to give up university to marry Christopher. Ever since then there had been constraint between them, a barrier that Zara could never afterwards cross. At the time she had put it down to their anger at having their plans and ambitions for her spoilt and she had half expected things to change once she had become successful, but they never had.

But she just *had* to know the truth, so she said abruptly, 'I met a man I used to know. His name is Heath Masterson. He told me that . . .' She broke off as her mother flinched and put her hand up to her mouth.

'So it *was* true,' Zara said in little more than a whisper. 'You did lie to me.'

Her mother nodded miserably. 'I've been wanting to tell you for a long time, but your father wouldn't let me. I knew we'd done the wrong thing almost from the start, but your dad was so insistent; he so wanted you to go to university. He wanted you to have all the chances that we never had, you see.'

'So you lied to Heath and intercepted his letters and phone calls?'

'Yes,' Mrs Layston admitted. 'Your father said it would be better to make a clean break. He said you'd soon forget him once the man had gone to America. But you didn't, though, did you?'

'No, I never forgot him.'

'I thought not. That's why it never worked with Christopher wasn't it?'

Zara nodded numbly. 'Yes, I was always in love with Heath.'

Her mother reached up to touch her hand, but then let it fall again. 'I'm sorry, Zara, I really am. If only we could go back. . .' Her face brightened. 'But you say you've met him again; perhaps now . . .'

'No,' Zara said shortly. 'It's too late. Much too late.' She lifted her head, looking round the room. She had insisted on buying a better house for her parents as soon as she could afford it, and it had hurt when they had been so reluctant to take that and the other things she had given them. But now she understood why; they had felt guilty, and it is difficult to take things from someone to whom you feel guilt.

Turning, she walked towards the door, but the older woman caught her arm. 'Don't go. We did it for the best, we really did! We couldn't see how it would turn out. We just wanted you to finish your education, get a degree.' She bit her lip and said pleadingly. 'We did it because we loved you, Zara. Please don't cut us out now.'

Zara gave a short, hollow laugh. 'The things people do in the name of love!' she said harshly. 'No, I won't cut you out of my life. Why should I, when you're all I'll ever have?'

On the drive back to London she sat huddled in the back of the car, cold and dispirited, realising that she had lost the man she loved not once but twice. Fate had given her the chance to find happiness again, and she had ruined it with her determination to be avenged on Heath. Like her mother said, if only you could go back. Zara shut her eyes, too wretched to cry. She would do what she could to put things right financially for Heath, but the future stretched in front of her long and bleak and empty, even her pride in Panache turned to dust and ashes.

She directed the driver to take her back to the office, but when they got there it seemed to take all her strength to get out of the car and go in. The driver put his hand under her elbow, looking at her anxiously. 'Are you all right, Miss Layston?'

Somehow she managed to nod and give him the travesty of a smile. 'Fine, thank you.'

Mac was equally anxious when she walked into the office, looking at her sharply and saying, 'I thought you were going to see your parents?'

'I did. I went there this morning.' She sat down at her desk and automatically picked up a pen.

'You're not going to work, are you? You look terrible. You ought to be at home in bed.'

'Stop mothering me, Mac, and go away. I have some letters to write.'

He looked at her for a moment, then handed her an envelope. 'This came for you this morning, by hand. It's marked private and confidential.'

Zara took it from him, glancing at the envelope, but becoming very still as she recognised Heath's thick, purposeful handwriting. 'Th-thanks.'

She waited for Mac to go, but he hesitated and then burst out, 'Zara, if anyone's upset you—if you want to talk about it or need help—well, you know you can rely on me, or any of us, don't you?'

Lifting her head, Zara looked at him with lacklustre eyes that slowly warmed as she realised that she didn't have just her parents but loyal friends too. She nodded. 'Yes, I know. Thanks, Mac. But I—I can't talk about it. I—I've done something terrible and I have to try and put it right.'

When he had gone, she slowly opened the envelope and took out the letter inside. It was very short and terse, saying: 'In view of your letter and our conversation yesterday, I have no option but to tender my resignation as Managing Director of Masterads. I can only hope that from somewhere you will now find the decency to keep on the rest of Masterads' staff and not take your insane desire for revenge out on them, too.'

Some conversation! Zara thought, remembering, and suddenly wondered if Heath was right, that she was mad. Biting her lip hard, she pulled a sheet of headed notepaper towards her and, after a moment's thought, began to write. She wrote several letters, one to her stockbroker, another to her fellow directors of Panache, a third to her solicitor and the last and most important, to Heath. Then she went to the safe and took out the Masterad shares she had bought and put them in a large envelope together with the letter to Heath. The other letters she put on top of her desk, but after hesitating for quite some time she decided she could do no other than to take the one to Heath herself.

Mac had been hovering in his office, but she managed to slip out when he wasn't looking and took a taxi to the Masterads agency. She gave her name to the receptionist and stood in the lobby waiting, wondering if Heath would ever consent to see her. But she was kept only a short while before she was shown into his office. It was a light and airy room, with the first sun that they had had that spring shining through the big windows. There was a desk in the middle of the room and a big map table over by the window, both of which were piled with boxes and papers as Heath packed to leave. He had his jacket off, the cuffs of his shirt turned up as he worked, his hair a little untidy as if he had run his hand through it several times. One of his staff was with him when she was shown in, but Heath said a curt, 'Excuse us, will you?' and the man went away and left them alone.

Heath gave her a sneering look. 'Come to take over already? Or just to make sure that I get out as quickly as possible?'

The words and the tone cut deep, but Zara betrayed it only by a tightening of her lips. 'No.' She shook her head. 'I came to—apologise. I went to see my mother this morning. She—verified what you said.' She expected Heath to say something, but he just looked at her stony-faced, and she went on, 'And I brought you this,' holding out the letter.

After a moment's hesitation Heath took it from her and tore it open, his eyes running swiftly over the letter and the contents. Then he said scathingly, 'So you refuse to accept my resignation, but you must know I can't afford to buy these shares back from you at the price you paid for them.'

'I'm not asking you to pay for them. I'm giving them to you.'

'And do you really think I'd accept them?' He threw the shares on to the desk. 'I don't need your charity, Zara. I can build another agency just as good as this one. You can even have *my* Masterads' shares. I want no part in anything that you're concerned with,' he added disparagingly.

'It isn't charity! They rightfully belong to you. And—and I have no use for them any more. Please take them.'

Heath stared into her white face, seeing the dark, bruising shadows around her eyes, and the drawn look of her cheeks and mouth as if she had lost weight suddenly. 'Why did you bring these here yourself?'

'I—I felt I had to. That I owed it to you.'

His face hardened. 'You owe me a hell of a lot more than that, you spiteful little cat!'

Zara's hands balled into tight, nail-pinching fists. 'Yes, I know. And I know that I can never make it up to you. You have the right to call me anything you want.'

His lips curled contemptuously. 'So you're into masochism too, are you?'

Her slim body trembled and she closed her eyes tightly for a moment. Then she opened them and said stammeringly, 'There—there was another reason why I came. You—you said . . . in the Bahamas you said that you—wanted me.'

'Well?' Heath demanded, his eyes fixed intently on her face as she struggled for words.

'So—so I came to give you that, too.'

'Yourself?'

'*Yes.*' She stood gazing at the floor, unable to meet his eyes, her hands twisting nervously together as she waited for him to speak.

'But how noble of you,' said Heath in mocking scorn. 'To sacrifice yourself as an act of atonement. I've never known anyone whose emotions were on such a grand scale: hate, revenge, remorse. But don't worry, Zara, you don't have to debase yourself by submitting your body to me. I can survive without being an altar for your penitence.'

She stared at him, unable to believe that he didn't want her, even if only to take his own revenge. 'You don't understand,' she said with sudden fierceness, her eyes pleading. 'I *want* you to make love to me—I—I want to know what it would have been like.'

Heath's body stiffened as he stared at her, then he

lunged forward and picked up the shares lying on the desk. 'So that's what these are for, is it?' he demanded harshly. 'To buy me!' And he threw them violently across the room.

'No!' She put her hands up to protect herself as he came striding round the desk. 'No, you don't understand.'

'On the contrary I understand all too well.' He towered over her, big and murderously angry, his voice savage as he said, 'Get out of here! Get out before I forget that you're only a psychotic little fool and I give you the hiding you deserve!'

Zara looked at him desperately, shaking her head and trying to speak. But then suddenly tears came into her eyes and flowed down her face and she turned and ran.

She bumped into people as she sped into the street and a car had to swerve violently to avoid her as she ran blindly across the road, but she didn't even notice. Her breath was coming in great gulps and her head was pounding unbearably. Her legs felt weak and she leaned up against a wall, shaking violently. People looked at her as they passed and one or two hesitated, but no one offered help. Brushing the tears away a little, Zara managed to look around and go to the kerb to hail a taxi, subsiding into it as she went home. The porter called out to her as she ran past his desk, but she fled up the stairs to the sanctuary of her flat, slamming the door behind her and throwing herself on the bed to sob convulsively.

The pent-up tears of many unhappy years overcame her as she lay there in abject wretchedness, and she didn't even hear the phone ringing or, half an hour or so later, the sound of her doorbell. This was followed by someone banging on her door, but she wasn't aware of that either. Five minutes later, Heath and the porter, with the master key in his hand, hurried in. Heath flung open her bedroom door, but stopped short when he saw her lying there. Then he heard her crying and saw no empty bottle of pills and his body relaxed. Turning to the porter, he said, 'It's all right, I'll take care of her. Thanks for your help.'

When the porter had gone Heath walked over to stand beside the bed and said drily, 'Feeling sorry for yourself, Zara?'

A sob caught in her throat and she stiffened, her hand clutching at the pillow. With a supreme effort she stifled her tears and sat up with her back to him. 'How—how did you get in here?'

'I persuaded the porter to open the door. The people at your office were worried about you. They said that you'd left a letter on your desk saying you were going away. They were afraid you might do something stupid—like killing yourself. Which, when you come to think of it, is the kind of thing a coward like you would do.'

Zara's face tightened and she stopped crying. 'So why you?'

'They seemed to think that your—emotional state was something to do with me and that I ought to deal with it.'

'Well, now you've dealt with it,' she said as evenly as she could, but a shudder ran through her as she added, 'Now you can go away and forget about me.'

Heath walked round the bed so that he could see her face. 'But what guarantee have I got that you won't swallow a bottle of sleeping pills when I'm out of the way?'

'I won't. I promise I won't.'

He gave a disbelieving laugh. 'You made me a promise once before, but you didn't keep it.'

'But that was before I knew ...' She stopped wretchedly. 'Look. I have no intention of committing suicide. As you said, I'm a coward. I'm not that brave.'

'And your letter?'

'It meant exactly what I said. I'm going away.'

'Where?'

She shrugged helplessly. 'I don't know. Africa, India, somewhere like that. Somewhere where I can work and perhaps do some good. Somewhere I can perhaps learn to be able to live with myself again. Find myself.' There was a note of despair in her voice and she looked down at the floor, her shoulders sagging.

Heath looked at her for a long moment and then said, 'Why should you do that? If it's anyone's fault it's your parents'. They were the ones who lied to us both and made us part in the first place. And it was because of their lies that you began to hate me, wasn't it?'

She shook her head. 'But I shouldn't have tried to get even with you.'

'No, you shouldn't, but when people are hurt it's human nature to want to hurt back.' Heath paused, and in a strained voice said, 'Why did you ask me to make love to you this afternoon?'

Zara stiffened. 'I thought—you wanted me.' He didn't speak and after a moment she said, 'No, that isn't true, is it? I thought of all those wasted years, all those nights I wished it was you I was in bed with. And I wanted to know, just once, what it would really have been like.' Her voice faded and she bit her lip. 'I'm sorry, I expect you find that—repellent after what I did to you.'

'No, I don't find you repellent,' Heath said softly. 'I loved you, too, remember? It hurt like hell when I heard that you'd married someone else and I thought that you hadn't really cared about me. But I could understand that because you were so young and I got over it—had to. But this time, when you stood there and told me how you'd lied to me and gone behind my back . . .'

Zara stood up agitatedly and walked into the sitting-room. 'Yes, you have every right to hate me now.'

'You told me only two days ago that you were in love with me,' he reminded her as he followed her in. 'Were you lying to me then?'

Fresh tears filled her eyes and she lifted a hand to brush them away. 'I'm sorry, I haven't cried for—for such a long time; now I can't seem to stop.'

Coming round to stand in front of her, Heath said, his voice harsh again, 'I asked you a question.'

Zara blinked and looked around like a cornered animal, but realised there was no escape and nodded. 'Yes, it was true. I don't think I ever really stopped loving you, not in all those long years.' Her head came up, her chin tilting defiantly. 'So now you have *your* weapon of revenge, don't you? You know I'm at your mercy and . . .'

'Zara.' He reached out and caught hold of her. 'Just

shut up, will you?' Then he stooped and picked her up in his arms.

'What are you doing?' she asked dazedly.

'What I should have done seven years ago. I'm going to take you to bed and make love to you.'

'But—but you can't want to,' she protested as he shouldered the bedroom door open and carried her inside.

'You crazy idiot,' Heath said thickly. 'Of course I want to. You're all I ever wanted from the first moment I met you.'

She stared at him, a wild, almost unimaginable hope in her heart. 'Are you ... do you mean you—you still love me? Even after ...'

'Always,' he said huskily as he put her down. 'No matter what.' Cupping her face with his hands, he said urgently, 'Don't cry, my darling. Don't ever cry again.' And then he kissed her with deep, aching longing, taking her mouth with the fierce hunger of a starving man. Zara gave a little moan of joy and thankfulness and sagged against him, but his growing passion soon made her respond as she put her arms round his neck and kissed him fervently in return.

His hands went to the zip of her dress, pulling it down in urgent haste, and then it was off her shoulders and Heath was kissing her neck, her throat. The dress fell to the floor and Zara stepped out of it, her breath quickening as he kissed her with wild passion, murmuring endearments against her mouth, sending her into an ascending spiral of pleasure. The rest of her clothes seemed to melt from her body, revealing her to his eyes and the exquisite torment of his caresses. His mouth, his hands, grew tremblingly eager as he avidly explored her, until she was moaning with heat and desire.

Picking her up, Heath kissed her as he carried her to the bed and put her in it. Zara clung to him, her body arching towards him and she gave a cry of protest when he took her hands from round his neck. 'Yes, my sweet, in just a moment.'

He was back very soon, lying beside her between the cool sheets. His arms reached out and drew her to him and for the first time she felt the heady, sensuous pleasure of his skin against her own. 'Oh, Heath! Oh, my love.' She gasped out his name on a rising tide of joy and excitement, her breath hot and panting as he held her close against him. 'I love you so much.'

'And I you, my darling, my love.' He kissed her again, his lips like burning brands against her skin as he moved down the bed to explore her quivering body. She moaned with tormented pleasure as he caressed her breasts, her fingers digging into his shouders. But it was too exquisite, such sweet torture. Zara couldn't stand it any longer and tore herself free, caught his head and kissed his mouth in greedy passion, aflame with an urgent need that made her almost fight to be near him. Heath's arms came round her and for a few moments she lay on top of him, their legs entwined as they kissed with savage abandon, each taking the other's mouth in frantic feverish need, their bodies hot, and wet with perspiration, their breath panting gasps of animal desire.

And then he swung her underneath him again, was lifting himself up on his elbows, his hard body probing hers. Zara gasped and went suddenly rigid, her hands holding him off. 'Zara?' he gasped out her name on a wild, questioning note and looked down at her hot flushed face.

'I—I've wanted you for so long. Waited for so many years. But now—now I'm afraid.'

Putting his hand on her damp forehead, he gently pushed aside her hair, his hand trembling. 'Don't ever be afraid. Because this is right, this is where you belong. It was the past that was wrong, not this. And it will be wonderful, my darling, now and always, because we love each other and because we've waited so long.'

For a moment she stared up at him, but then her hands went to his shoulders. 'Yes, oh, yes!' And she lifted her body to accept him.

Heath kissed her ardently again, his excitement at fever pitch, his body thrusting forward as he took her in an explosion of ecstasy that buried the past as it lifted them both to the heights of climactic pleasure. They had found each other again, and now, in the gradually darkening room, they pledged their bodies in a physical and emotional union that cleansed away blame and deceit, vengeance and pain, until they fell asleep in each other's arms, knowing that their future together was safe and assured.

Harlequin Presents

Coming Next Month

1047   RECKLESS   Amanda Carpenter
A routine assignment to South America turns into a nightmare when Leslie's flight is hijacked. She draws on all her strength to save fellow journalist Scott Bennett, only to discover the real test is of her ability to love again.

1048   STRIKE AT THE HEART   Emma Darcy
Sunny King is everything Jackie Mulholland disapproves of: rich, reckless and overwhelmingly arrogant. So she's disturbed by the attraction he seems to hold for her two young sons. She's even more disturbed by her own attraction to him.

1049   CARLISLE PRIDE   Leigh Michaels
Brooke has more than her share of pride. It was pride that made her break her engagement to Ty Marshall after finding him in her stepmother's arms; and it's pride that now makes her refuse to sell Oakley Manor...but refusing Ty again will cost more than pride.

1050   TAGGART'S WOMAN   Carole Mortimer
To inherit her rightful share of the family airline business, Heather is forced to marry her late father's partner, Daniel Taggart. For Heather the arrangement seems a little like hell—and heaven.

1051   TRUE ENCHANTER   Susan Napier
Joanna's not impressed by the superficial glamour of the film world, which is why she's the perfect chaperone for her actress niece. But she's not what director Richard Marlow expects. She can see right through him, as he does her. Have they both met their match?

1052   OPEN TO INFLUENCE   Frances Roding
A girl on her own, hopelessly in love with her married boss and without a job because of it, is hardly the ideal guardian for an orphaned three year old. So Rosemary is in no position to refuse Nicholas Powers, even if it means giving up a life—and love—of her own.

1053   BROKEN SILENCE   Kate Walker
When Jill negotiates her wages as a temporary nanny to Luke Garrett's small son, she doesn't bargain for the claim her employer makes on her own heart. She should have.

1054   THIS MAN'S MAGIC   Stephanie Wyatt
By asking her father for an introduction to Lucas Armory, Sorrel starts a chain of events that turns her life upside down. For Luke doesn't believe she's Felix Valentine's daughter, and worse, he accuses her of stealing his company's latest jewelry designs.

Available in January wherever paperback books are sold, or through Harlequin Reader Service:

In the U.S.
901 Fuhrmann Blvd.
P.O. Box 1397
Buffalo, N.Y. 14240-1397

In Canada
P.O. Box 603
Fort Erie, Ontario
L2A 5X3

*Coming Soon
from Harlequin . . .*

GIFTS FROM THE HEART

**Watch for it
in February**

HEART-1
February 88

Take 4 books & a surprise gift FREE

SPECIAL LIMITED-TIME OFFER

Mail to **Harlequin Reader Service**®

In the U.S.	In Canada
901 Fuhrmann Blvd.	P.O. Box 609
P.O. Box 1394	Fort Erie, Ontario
Buffalo, N.Y. 14240-1394	L2A 5X3

YES! Please send me 4 free Harlequin Romance® novels and my free surprise gift. Then send me 8 brand-new novels every month as they come off the presses. Bill me at the low price of $1.99 each*—an 11% saving off the retail price. There are no shipping, handling or other hidden costs. There is no minimum number of books I must purchase. I can always return a shipment and cancel at any time. Even if I never buy another book from Harlequin, the 4 free novels and the surprise gift are mine to keep forever.   118 BPR BP7F

*Plus 89¢ postage and handling per shipment in Canada.

Name _____ (PLEASE PRINT)

Address _____ Apt. No. _____

City _____ State/Prov. _____ Zip/Postal Code _____

This offer is limited to one order per household and not valid to present subscribers. Price is subject to change.   DOR-SUB-1D

ATTRACTIVE, SPACE SAVING BOOK RACK

Display your most prized novels on this handsome and sturdy book rack. The hand-rubbed walnut finish will blend into your library decor with quiet elegance, providing a practical organizer for your favorite hard-or soft-covered books.

Only $9.95

Approximately 16" x 8" when assembled

Assembles in seconds!

To order, rush your name, address and zip code, along with a check or money order for $10.70* ($9.95 plus 75¢ postage and handling) payable to *Harlequin Reader Service*:

Harlequin Reader Service
Book Rack Offer
901 Fuhrmann Blvd.
P.O. Box 1396
Buffalo, NY 14269-1396

Offer not available in Canada.

BKR-1A

*New York and Iowa residents add appropriate sales tax.

Harlequin Intrigue

In October
Watch for the new look of

Harlequin Intrigue
... because romance can be quite an adventure!

Each time, Harlequin Intrigue brings you great stories, mixing a contemporary, sophisticated romance with the surprising twists and turns of a puzzler ... romance with "something more."

Plus ...
in next month's publications of Harlequin Intrigue we offer you the chance to win one of four mysterious and exciting weekends. Don't miss the opportunity! Read the October Harlequin Intrigues!

J-INT-R